DUELING MINDS

The Wizard stared at Blade over a hooked nose. Wearing a black velvet tunic with slashed and puffed sleeves, carrying a dagger with a silver hilt, the Wizard reminded Blade of some great nobleman of the Italian Renaissance. He was a man who could admire an exquisite statue one day and order a dozen men out for execution the next.

Then the Wizard spoke—in the Rentoran language, with an accent that reminded Blade of something from Home Dimension.

A moment later Blade sensed a message passing into his mind, filling it like an echoing shout in a cave.

"Open your thoughts to me," was the message. "Open them, and let me know them. I am not your enemy."

Fortunately, Blade had been warned he might be facing telepathy and other paranormal powers. And he knew he had to resist. The Wizard would not stop at reading Blade's thoughts. He would plant his own ideas in Blade's mind until he had gained total control.

Blade began his mental duel with the Wizard: His first thought was a defiant shout against the Wizard's statement, "I am not your enemy."

You are a liar! Blade mentally shouted. *You are a liar! You are a liar!*

The Blade Series:

HEROIC FANTASY SERIES

28

An incredible time-space journey to Dimension X!

RICHARD BLADE

WIZARD OF RENTORO
by Jeffrey Lord

PINNACLE BOOKS • LOS ANGELES

BLADE #28: WIZARD OF RENTORO

Copyright © 1978 by Lyle Kenyon Engel

An original Pinnacle Books edition, published for the first time anywhere.

First printing, August 1978

ISBN: 0-523-40206-6

Cover illustration by John Alvin

Printed in the United States of America

PINNACLE BOOKS, INC.
2029 Century Park East
Los Angeles, California 90067

WIZARD OF RENTORO

Chapter 1

Dawn broke over London as Richard Blade's train pulled into the station. It was a dawn that promised a clear, sunny day, rare for London at this time of the year. It was a pity, thought Blade, that he'd been spending the morning sleeping and the afternoon far below the Tower of London. By the time sunset flamed over London, he would be far away from the city, from Britain, from the whole world.

He would be somewhere in Dimension X, the infinite unknown on the other side of a barrier made by his own brain and his own senses. When that brain was linked to Lord Leighton's computer, when those senses were twisted out of their normal shape, the barrier vanished.

He'd crossed into Dimension X twenty-seven times since the day Lord Leighton first linked his brain to a computer and opened the door to Dimension X. Each journey brought new dangers to test Blade's skill and strength to the limit. He'd escaped from some of those dangers by the narrowest of margins. Sooner or later, he would not escape at all, unless someone else could be found—someone able to travel into Dimension X and return to Britain alive and sane. For the time being, that someone did not exist. Richard Blade was the only living human being who could cross from Home Dimension into Dimension X and return without destroying his mind or his body.

Yet whatever the danger to him, he could not end his travels into Dimension X. Out there lay resources and knowledge beyond price. The exploration of Dimension X had to continue, whatever the risk to Blade, whatever the frustrations when a possible discovery turned out to be nothing, whatever their ignorance of the dangers. It had to continue, in the hope that Project Dimension X would someday justify all the blood, sweat, knowledge, and money that had been poured into it since it began. The stakes were too great.

1

Blade no longer expected that happy day to come soon. At times he wondered if he'd live to see it. Blade didn't let himself dwell on that much. He had too much self-control to worry about things that couldn't be helped. He also had too strong a sense of duty. Britain could not do without his services—therefore he would go on serving. This sense of duty had taken him to every corner of the world as the top field agent for the secret intelligence agency MI6. Now it was taking him to even stranger places.

In any case, if Blade was frustrated, what about J and Lord Leighton? J had been Blade's chief in MI6 and now worked for the security of Project Dimension X. He loved Blade as a son, yet accepted seeing Blade hurled off into the unknown time after time. He was also nearly seventy. He might not live to see the Project bear fruit, even if he never took any trip more dangerous than a taxi ride through the streets of London!

And Lord Leighton? The computer that opened the door to Dimension X was his creation. Project Dimension X was his brainchild, absorbing the last years of his life and career. Leighton was ten years older than J, his spine twisted into a hunchback, his legs twisted by polio, what little hair he had left snow-white. His scientific career had earned him several fortunes and the right to a peaceful retirement. Yet here he was, brilliant mind and twisted body both hard at work, with little to show for it so far.

Blade at least could forget the frustrations and failures of the Project in the grimly simple business of trying to stay alive in Dimension X. Lord Leighton and J weren't so fortunate. They had the Project staring them in the face every waking minute, with nothing to distract them. Perhaps, thought Blade, he was the lucky man after all.

Blade took a taxi from the station to his flat, undressed, ate breakfast in his dressing gown, and slept until noon. Then he took a shower, shaved, and pulled on the first clothes that came to hand.

There was no point in dressing up for a trip to Dimension X. He always began the trips wearing nothing but a coat of foul-smelling black grease and a loincloth, and ended them wearing nothing at all. All the clothes he was pulling on now had to do was keep him from getting wet, cold, or arrested for indecent exposure until he got to the Tower.

The taxi crept through London's traffic and deposited Blade at the Tower. The grim-faced Special Branch men who guarded the entrance to the underground complex checked Blade's identification and passed him through. The elevator plunged two hundred feet down in a few seconds, and the long echoing corridor led him to the computer section.

J met him at the far end of the corridor. When they were at the door leading to the main computer, out of earshot of the technicians and programmers, the older man turned to Blade. "The Prime Minister wasn't very happy about your report on the American trip," he said.

"I didn't write it to make the old—the man happy," said Blade shortly. Actually, there was no point in being harsh. The Prime Minister was another man doing his best and enduring a great deal of trouble. Without his efforts in providing money and discouraging inquisitive members of Parliament, Project Dimension X would long since have fallen apart.

"No, but he did have hopes that the Americans might be able to contribute more. I'm afraid he has the usual notion that in the American intelligence services money grows on trees and they can give it away by the barrel to any likely project."

Blade laughed and shook his head. He'd gone off to the United States with some of those same notions himself. He'd spent a working vacation, taking desert-survival and underwater-demolitions refresher training, looking over a few possible candidates for Project Dimension X, and generally keeping up his contacts in the American intelligence services. Parts of the month had been pleasant enough, but in the end he'd been disappointed.

"The CIA's too busy putting its own house in order to be very receptive to new and expensive projects," he said. "The money's there, but it would be like pulling teeth to get them to spend it on a British request.

"Even if they were willing to spend it, their internal security's below standard these days. By the time they'd come through with the money, somebody would have leaked everything to the press. Then Project Dimension X would be on national television, the front page of the *Washington Post*, and God knows where else."

J winced at the idea. After a moment he asked, "What about approaches to some of the other American agencies—

3

the military ones, for example? They aren't under such close examination by the press."

Blade recognized J's tone. The older man was not seeking information on a matter of which he was ignorant. What he wanted was Blade's point of view, on a matter where the facts were already known. J had been in intelligence work for the better part of half a century, and knew as well as any man alive how much more there was to it than simple facts. A great many of J's friends and allies were alive because he'd gone beyond the facts. Almost as many enemies were dead.

"No, they aren't," said Blade. "But that won't help us. The CIA is just as jealous of its status as ever, in spite of all its troubles. If we approached—oh, the Defense Intelligence Agency, for example—without giving the CIA at least the chance to turn us down, there'd be the devil to pay! We could kiss good-bye any hope of American cooperation for about the next five years. We don't want to have to wait that long, I think."

"No," said J. "We don't. But we are going to have to give the Americans a miss for a while. That puts us back to square one as far as finding new people are concerned. Our own agencies and services have already been gone over with a fine-toothed comb. I'm damned if I can see any point in trying them again, and I can't see the Prime Minister supporting it, either." He sighed, and for a brief moment he looked more than his age.

Blade stood in silent sympathy. Once again he couldn't help feeling that perhaps he was the lucky man in the Project. In another hour he would be striking out across some unknown land far off in Dimension X. J would still be here in Britain, sweating over irritated Prime Ministers, the internal politics of American intelligence agencies, and a dozen other administrative problems.

Any of them would have quickly driven Blade mad. He was not an administrator. A desk could never be his home. He was a natural adventurer, born into the wrong century. Yet somehow he'd found the one job which he could do better than any other human being. That was better luck than Blade would have believed any man could enjoy—certainly better luck than J's or Lord Leighton's.

The door in front of the two men hissed open, and Lord Leighton's gnome-like face peered out at them. His glasses were shoved up on his wrinkled forehead, and for a moment he didn't seem to recognize them. Then he pulled his glasses down into position and gave his usual brief smile of welcome.

In silence J and Blade followed the scientist into the room that was Leighton's private preserve. All around them the gray crackle-finished consoles of the master computer towered toward the bare rock of the ceiling. In the exact center of the room a grimly functional metal chair squatted inside a transparent glass booth. That chair was the beginning and the end for Blade's trips into Dimension X.

Blade left the other two men. J sat down on the folding spectator seat, while Leighton took his position by the main control panel. Blade went to the changing room carved into the rock wall, pulled the door shut behind him, and began stripping off his clothes.

When he was naked, he picked up the pot of dark grease from one corner and began smearing it over every square inch of his skin. It had the consistency of suet pudding mixed with well-rotted rabbit droppings, and smelled nearly as unpleasant. Blade would have been more than willing to leave it off, if it hadn't been for the danger of electrical burns. A frightening amount of current passed through his body as he was hurled into Dimension X. He would not run even the slightest risk of winding up fried like a chicken.

Blade finished smearing himself, knotted a loincloth about his waist, and stepped out of the changing room. Leighton was standing by the chair now, a bundle of wires and electrodes gripped in one surprisingly large and strong hand. The scientist must be more eager than usual to see me off, thought Blade. Well, he can hardly be more eager than I am. At this point the last of Blade's tension always faded away, leaving behind only a great impatience to be off on his next adventure.

Blade sat down in the chair, feeling the chill rubber of the back and seat against his bare skin. He leaned back and started breathing quickly and deeply, filling his whole system with oxygen. The doctors of the Project had the notion that if he hyperventilated before the computer gripped him, it might help prevent the splitting headache he usually felt after arriving in Dimension X. The headache always went away within a few minutes, but during those few minutes it was often so painful that Blade could hardly move. It would be an advantage to be ready for action the moment he awoke in Dimension X. Only a small advantage, to be sure—but Blade's training and experience had taught him how much even small advantages could mean to survival.

Lord Leighton practically ran in circles around Blade, attaching the cobra-headed metal electrodes to every part of Blade's body. From each electrode a colored wire led off into the bowels of the computer. By the time Leighton finished, Blade sprouted wires from the crown of his head to the tips of his toes. He looked like the victim of a mad scientist in a low-grade horror film.

Well, Lord Leighton certainly looked enough like a mad scientist to be cast for the part. There were probably some people who thought he actually *was* mad. Certainly he could be eccentric, stubborn, outrageous, and totally impossible to get along with. Blade wondered how many of the white hairs on J's head had been added by having to deal with the scientist. Probably quite a few. But it was worth it. Lord Leighton might hold a large part of the future of the human race in his mind and hand.

Blade saw the room around him appearing with unnatural clarity and felt his head beginning to swim. He knew that he'd done enough deep breathing, stopped, and let himself relax. As he did, Leighton stepped to the main control panel and pulled the red master switch down to the bottom of its slot.

A buzzing started in Blade's head, then swelled to a screaming roar. It sounded like a jet plane winding up for takeoff, and Blade half expected the room to start vibrating savagely. It seemed unnatural that there should be so much noise with no movement.

In the next moment the room tilted up on end, as if a giant hand were gripping it and heaving. Blade saw Leighton and J standing frozen as the floor tilted, until they were standing at such an angle that Blade expected them to fall down out of sight. The floor tilted still more and the whole room turned upside down—Lord Leighton, J, the control panel, the computer consoles, Blade in his chair, everything. Now Lord Leighton and J seemed to be hanging head downward, like bats from the ceiling of a cave. The roaring swelled until Blade wanted to scream at the tearing agony in his eardrums.

Suddenly the noise died, and in the same moment the chair detached itself from the inverted floor and plunged downward, carrying Blade with it. He plunged into a vast windy darkness that suddenly spread beneath him. The darkness swallowed him, the wind howled about him, and a numbing chill began to gnaw at his fingers and toes.

The fall through the darkness went on and on, and the cold began to work through Blade's skin into his internal organs. Then there was no longer darkness below. A vast plain spread out in all directions, a plain made of shimmering green light. In a hundred places vast mouths gaped open, mouths with lips of dancing golden fire and blazing silver teeth. Now they seemed to be aware of Blade and they began opening and shutting furiously.

Blade tried to twist in midair, to divert his fall and plunge into the green light instead of into one of the mouths. He failed. A mouth yawned wide directly below him, silver teeth flashed past him, he felt a moment of searing heat as deadly as the cold before—then he no longer felt anything at all.

Chapter 2

The first thing Blade felt was rain on his bare skin and wet grass under him. He opened his eyes, then realized with delight that his head was not throbbing with pain. There was a faint ache, rather like a mild hangover, but nothing that would slow him down even slightly. The deep breathing—or *something*—had worked.

That was pure good news, like anything else learned about Dimension X or ways of reaching it in one piece. Exploring Dimension X often seemed like trying to assemble a jigsaw puzzle with half the pieces missing. Now he'd just found one more piece.

Blade rose, stretched his arms and legs, and did a quick series of limbering-up exercises. When he'd finished, he felt ready to look around him and see where he'd landed.

Overhead was a sky of featureless gray clouds, trailing cotton-wool tufts of mist all the way to the ground. A fine rain was still falling.

Blade was standing in ankle-deep grass by the edge of a shallow drainage ditch now filled to the brim with muddy water. On either side of him rose thick tangles of vines. The leaves were long and thin with a white stripe down the middle. The fruit was the size and shape of grapes, but bright blue.

The vines rose ten feet high on either side of Blade and stretched away in both directions. In front of him they seemed to go on forever, until they vanished in the rain and the mist. He turned, and saw the vines ending fifty feet away at a waist-high wall of roughly dressed stone. He started walking toward it.

The earth underfoot was rich, black, and clinging. Judging from the smell that reached Blade's nostrils, it had been recently manured. Along the edge of the drainage ditch the earth was turning to mud, and several times Blade sank up to his ankles. The grass between the vines had been weeded recently and in places showed signs of careful cutting. Blade saw nothing he could hope to use as a weapon.

He was halfway to the wall when he heard a loud metallic honk from somewhere out of sight. The damp air distorted the sound so that it was hard to be sure where it came from.

Several more honks sounded in a ragged chorus, followed by unmistakable human voices shouting in wordless anger and the soft squishing of hooves in mud. The sounds were coming closer. Blade went down on his belly and crawled the rest of the distance to the wall on his hands and knees. From the cover of the wall and the vines, Blade watched the travelers ride past him.

There were seven of them, all mounted on animals that looked like thick-legged antelopes covered with long white hair. The heads were broad and slab-sided, with large eyes set well to either side. From in front of each hairless pink ear a two-foot horn jutted forward. The points were sharp as needles, and the horns of the lead rider's mount were gilded.

The leader himself was dressed in armor that might have come straight out of some museum's medieval or Renaissance collection. It was mostly plate, with a sort of skirt of chain mail and more mail in the armpits to let the wearer move his arms freely. The helmet was a massive affair, almost completely round, with a hinged visor of close-set metal bars. The visor was raised, and the face it revealed was olive-hued and heavily mustached.

The man was carrying a lance in his right hand and controlling his mount with the left. From his belt hung a sword in an elaborately decorated scabbard of leather and metal. On his saddle was slung a triangular shield about three feet long and two feet wide. It was covered with red leather, and on the leather was painted an elaborate heraldic device in green, white, and gold. Before Blade could make out any details of the device, the leader was passing out of sight.

The six riders who followed the leader were less heavily equipped. They wore open-faced helmets, back and breast plates, mail skirts, and leather leggings tucked into high boots. Each one had a crossbow slung on his back and a sword or a mace at his belt. Three of them rode with falcon-like birds perched on gauntleted hands. The birds were white with golden-brown wings, their heads concealed in blue leather hoods.

9

On each breastplate was a smaller version of the device on the leader's shield. Blade was able to make it out as a wolf's head—mouth open, teeth bared, and red tongue licking out like a flame. Then the seven riders were past and out of Blade's sight.

Blade waited until the splashing and squelching of the animals' hooves faded almost into silence. Then he slipped over the wall and crouched beside the road. It hardly deserved the name—a yard-wide stretch of bare earth with a ditch on the far side. In spite of the ditch, the road was inches deep in water in many places.

Still, the road would be quicker than cutting through the vineyards and across fields, climbing over walls and risking encounters with farmers. Blade didn't expect he would have far to go. The men hadn't been on the road for long; otherwise their mounts would have been plastered with mud. Nor did they seem to be planning on any sort of long trip. They had no saddlebags on their mounts and no pack animals with them—nothing but their armor and weapons.

Somewhere not far away was a human settlement, possibly a castle matching the weapons and armor of these men. Blade would follow the riders to their destination and look the place over. If the people there looked reasonably friendly, he could introduce himself, dry off, and get food and clothing.

He hoped the people would be friendly. A night or two spent out in the rain wouldn't hurt him, not unless it grew much colder. But it would be a miserable experience, to be avoided if possible. Blade rose to his feet and started off after the riders.

The road wound back and forth between the stone wall on one side and the ditch on the other. Beyond the ditch was another wall, and beyond it a checkerboard of freshly plowed fields. They rose up a hillside until the mist and the clouds swallowed them.

Blade moved steadily along the road, as fast as he could without making too much noise or tiring himself. The mud splashed up with every step. He would have been coated up to his waist if the rain hadn't started coming down heavily enough to wash him clean.

He couldn't help thinking he must be a bizzarre sight, striding along this sodden road in such weather, as naked as the day he was born. He'd gotten used to looking strange after arriving in Dimension X, though, and anyone who replaced him in the Project would have to do the same.

After a while the rain began to slacken, and Blade thought he saw a hint of the mist lifting as well. The riders were long since out of earshot, but as far as he could tell they were still on the road. The rain hadn't completely washed out their hoofprints and there was no place they could have left the road to cut across country without leaving tracks.

Now the road curved sharply, vanishing around the rocky flank of a steep wooded hill. As Blade followed the road around to the right, he came to a small wooden bridge leading across the ditch. Beyond the ditch a flock of sheep milled about aimlessly. In the middle of the flock the slight form of a shepherd boy was sprawled on the ground. He lay on his back, his dark hair spread out around his head and his cap fallen to one side. His crook lay in three pieces beside him.

Blade ran across the bridge, crouching low and scanning the landscape for signs of movement. He noticed as he ran that some planks of the bridge were scarred and gouged by iron-shod hooves and that the ground on the far side bore a tangle of hoofprints. Some of the riders had come across the bridge only a few minutes before. They'd killed the shepherd boy, then apparently ridden away without doing anything to his flock—which made no sense.

Blade pushed through the sheep, who scattered with plaintive bleats. He knelt beside the shepherd and with relief discovered the boy was not dead. He had a nasty lump on his head and blood was seeping from a cut under one eye, but his limbs were straight and his chest rose and fell steadily. Blade stood up and started looking for shelter. The boy would come to no further harm if he could be dried off and warmed up.

Then an explosion of new sounds cut through the dying rain. Men and women were crying out in fear, children were screaming wildly, sheep, goats, and cattle were all bleating or lowing frantically. Other men were shouting angrily, and the hooves of fast-ridden animals splashed and thudded.

Blade had caught up with the riders. Somewhere over on the other side of the wooded hill, they were going into action. Whatever they were doing involved many more people than a single shepherd boy.

Blade drew the boy's cap over his face, then ran back across the bridge and out into the road.

Chapter 3

As Blade reached the road the uproar from beyond the hill seemed to double. There was a pitched battle, a wild panic, or both going on over there. Remembering the riders' crossbows, Blade changed his mind about following the road around the hill. Walking unarmed straight into whatever was going on would be a fine way of committing suicide and not much else.

Instead Blade ran on across the road, vaulted the wall, and started up the hill. The trees swallowed him before he'd gone a dozen paces but the cries and shouts still came loud and clear. He went up the hill with a rush, ignoring rocks that bruised his feet and thorn-laden branches that lashed across his skin. In places the slope was so steep he had to grip saplings or roots and haul himself upward. At last he reached the crest and ran to the nearest gap in the trees. He threw himself flat behind a spreading evergreen bush and peered down at the scene below.

Nestled in a hollow at the foot of the hill was a village— sixty or seventy houses, stables, barns, storehouses, a couple of inns, all arranged on either side of a single graveled street. The six men-at-arms were riding up and down that street at a canter, while their leader sat on his mount at one end of the street.

The leader's visor was still up and his face was turned toward the sky. He seemed totally deaf and blind to the uproar around him. He reminded Blade of nothing so much as a faithful dog sitting at his master's feet, waiting for a command. Where that command was going to come from, Blade couldn't imagine.

The men-at-arms, on the other hand, seemed to know exactly what they were doing and were grimly at work. They still had their bows slung, but their swords and maces danced in their hands. Blade saw one of them ride down a boy who

12

could not have been more than ten. The mace whistled down and Blade braced himself to see the child's head smashed to pulp. Then he saw the mace flash with frightening precision inches over the child's head, close enough to ruffle his dark hair. The boy missed a step and sprawled on the gravel, kicking and screaming hysterically, frightened into a fit but otherwise unhurt. The man-at-arms rode on without a backward glance at his victim.

Toward the other end of the village Blade saw a woman burst out of a doorway, trying to make a dash across the street. Two of the men-at-arms saw her and pulled their mounts around so violently Blade expected the animals to lose their footing on the wet gravel. If the men-at-arms went down, it would be easy for the villagers to surround them and take them prisoner or bash out their brains.

The white riding antelopes were too sure-footed. They reared, seemed to spin on their hind legs, then dashed toward the woman. One man rode between her and the houses on the far side of the street. The other swept in behind her, pulled his mount to a stop, and sprang down from the saddle. She whirled, mouth opening in a shrill scream. The man dropped his sword and punched the woman in the stomach hard enough to double her up. Then he grabbed her by the shoulders, threw her on her back on the gravel, pulled her skirts up to her waist, and went to work.

Four of the six men-at-arms raped the woman, and her screams floated up and down the village street. As the fourth man rose and began doing up his breeches, the remaining two rode out from behind a barn. One had a nude teenage girl slung across his saddle, her hands and feet bound and tied to his stirrups. The other had his crossbow cocked and aimed, and was herding ahead of him two husky young men, barefoot and stripped to the waist.

As the last two men-at-arms rode out into the street, a wild cry of rage exploded from one of the houses. A door flew open and a gray-haired man with a huge ax swinging in his hands burst into view. He took three steps, then the rider with the crossbow shifted his aim and fired. The bolt took the man in the leg and he went down with a howl of pain.

This seemed to snap the armored leader out of his trance. In a single fluid motion he lowered his lance and dug in his spurs. His mount leaped forward, spraying gravel. The lance dipped and plunged with terrible precision straight into the

13

center of the man's chest. He rose clear of the ground, impaled on the lance, as the leader swept on. Then the body slid free and thudded face down into the street. The leader pulled his mount around, wiped the blood from the lance point on the dead man's clothes, and rode back up the street. In a sharp voice he gave three orders the words of which Blade could not make out. Then his face turned up to the sky again and he fell back into his trance.

The man with the ax was the first and the last bit of resistance from the villagers. No one else did anything but scream or try to run a few steps as the men-at-arms swept back and forth through the village. Three more women writhed and cried out under the pounding bodies of the riders. A dozen more children were frightened into fits or fainting spells. Another young man was dragged out of a hut and bound with the first two. A second girl was stripped naked and thrown over a rider's saddle.

Then three of the men remounted and sat with crossbows at the ready. Of the other three, two began going into houses and barns and hauling out clothes, shoes, small articles of furniture, dishes, whatever seemed to come to hand. Some of it they smashed, some of it they trampled, some of it they just left lying on the ground where they threw it. The street began to look like a trash dump.

The third man-at-arms was the largest of all the riders, inches taller and broader than Blade himself. He wore a thick red beard and an ugly scar ran across his left cheek. He picked up the dead man's ax and strode up and down the street, taking swings at anything he felt like hitting. Porch beams split in two, doors fell off their hinges, fence rails were chopped into firewood.

At last the leader came out of his trance for a second time. He did not speak, but his quick gestures were so clear and precise that no words were needed. The three young men were each tied by the wrists to one of the stirrups. The dismounted men-at-arms scrambled into their saddles. The leader raised his lance high into the air and swung it in three slow circles. Then he spurred his mount forward and the men-at-arms did the same. All seven men rode out of the village at a brisk trot, the three young men trying desperately to keep their feet and the two unconscious women bouncing wildly. The red-bearded man brought up the rear. As he reached the end of the street he flung the ax down and spat on it. Then

14

all seven riders were vanishing into the grayness without a backward glance.

Blade wasted no time wondering what all this might mean. There were clothes, footgear, and perhaps weapons scattered all up and down the village street. He wanted to get down there and get himself clothed, shod, and armed before the villagers recovered and came out to gather up their possessions. The next village might be miles away and the daylight was beginning to fade.

Blade scrambled down the hill as fast as he dared go. He reached the end of the street before anyone came out of the houses. He darted from one heap of the villagers' possessions to another, scooping up whatever looked useful. He found baggy trousers, a woollen vest, a leather tunic, a belt, boots, three pairs of heavy stockings, a carving knife heavy enough to make a good weapon—

Now he came to a wicker basket and saw it full of loaves of hard gray bread. He scooped several into the vest and was just straightening up when a woman appeared in the doorway of a hut across the street.

"Heeee-ya!" she shrieked, waving her arms furiously at Blade. Her cry brought heads popping out of doors and windows all along the street. One man stepped out of a barn, holding a pitchfork. Several children picked up stones and clods of mud.

Blade wasted no more time in gathering up more equipment. Tucking his heavy bundle under his left arm, he held his right hand out in front of him, fingers spread.

This peaceful gesture was ignored. "Snake!" the woman screamed. "Dung-eating swine!" shouted someone else. The man with the pitchfork started toward Blade. Several stones and clods flew at Blade. One hit him in the shoulder. More men were stepping out of doorways, holding sticks, chair legs, and lengths of firewood.

Blade realized that his chances of making friends with the villagers were just about nonexistent. His chances of being killed, on the other hand, were very good and rapidly getting better. It was embarrassing to have to retreat from a village of half-armed, furious peasants, but it would be a great deal worse to be pulled down and torn to pieces by them.

Blade took three long steps to the fallen ax and picked it up. He whirled it around his head until it hissed in the air, and twisted his face into a ferocious glare. The men who'd

15

been edging toward him stopped. A number of heads popped hastily out of sight and a number of doors slammed. Blade swung the ax over his shoulder and broke into a run toward the far end of the village. Beyond it he could see the road winding away into the countryside. He didn't know what lay out there, but he knew that if he went the other way he'd be following the seven riders. He wanted to see as little as possible of the riders with the wolf's-head device until he knew a good deal more about them.

Blade plunged down the street and did not look back until he was well out into the countryside. More of the villagers were back out into the street and faint curses reached Blade's ears. He shrugged, turned, and ran on.

This time he did not stop running until the village was out of sight behind him. Then he picked out a pair of trousers and a vest that would fit him, pulled them on, tied the rest of his loot into a more manageable bundle, and moved on through the twilight that was settling down over the land.

Chapter 4

It was nearly dark before Blade found any sort of dry shelter. It was a woodcutter's hut, obviously abandoned for years but still almost intact. It was closer to the road than Blade would have liked, but he'd heard no signs of pursuit.

The boots he'd snatched up turned out to be three or four sizes too small. If he tried to walk a mile in them he'd be crippled for a week with blisters. He threw the boots into a corner and tried on the rest of the clothing. Some of it actually fitted, after he'd ripped a few seams here and there. This was a problem he was used to facing in Dimension X. Even in Home Dimension his massive frame—six feet one, two hundred and ten well-muscled pounds—was hard to clothe. In Dimension X, where people were often smaller, it was sometimes impossible.

Blade pulled on all three pairs of stockings and swept dead leaves into a rough bed. Then he lay back on the leaves and munched a loaf of bread while he considered what he'd seen.

The more he thought about it, the stranger it seemed. The seven riders were obviously highly trained, expert fighting men. In the face of the villagers' lack of resistance, they could have made a shambles of the place, looting, burning, slaughtering people right and left.

Yet what had they actually done? They'd kidnapped three men and two girls. They'd raped a few women, and frightened a good many children out of their wits. They'd done a lot of vandalism, but nothing that even these peasants couldn't make good in a few months. They'd only killed one man, although they'd obviously had the skill and weapons to kill fifty.

They must have had orders, Blade realized. Orders to take able-bodied prisoners, terrorize women and children, smash enough property to annoy everybody, but kill only when absolutely necessary. If that man hadn't come dashing out with the ax, he would probably be alive and drinking his beer tonight.

The riders had their orders. From whom? That was an entirely different question, and one not so easily answered. Blade remembered the leader sitting on his mount, eyes fixed on the sky, apparently lost in a trance. Had the man been waiting for orders? If so, how had he expected to receive them, doing nothing but sitting on his mount and staring up at the gray sky?

That helmet of his was roomy enough to hold a radio, but radio made no snese in a Dimension of peasant villages and riders in plate armor. Maybe he'd been seeing some signal from outside Blade's field of vision. Maybe—

Maybe it was time to stop guessing! This Dimension contained extremely well-trained fighting men, who seemed to follow the orders of some distant master. Both the men and their master could be dangerous enemies or powerful friends.

That was all Blade could know for the moment. He would just have to do what he'd done in a dozen other places, both in Home Dimension and in Dimension X. Watch his step and his tongue, guard his back, and keep his eyes and ears open. It was an effective prescription for survival. If it hadn't been, Richard Blade would have been dead many times over.

Blade finished the first loaf and ate half of a second. The bread was lumpy, coarse gray stuff, sour, damp, and heavy. It lay like a brick on his stomach, but almost any sort of food gave some energy. There'd be no shortage of water, either, not with this rain.

Blade pulled the blanket tightly around himself and lay down to get some sleep.

The rain must have stopped well before dawn. Blade awoke in full daylight, with sun flooding the forest and the only sound the drip of water from the leaves and needles. He found a spring only a few yards away, drank, shouldered his ax, and moved on.

In daylight he could get a better look at the clothes he'd snatched up from the village and roughly pulled on. No two garments were the same size, the same color, the same material or texture. He looked like a scarecrow run away from its field, a tramp dressed in stolen castoffs—or perhaps a footloose woodcutter, with no home but the forest and no roof but the sky. A footloose woodcutter, exactly the sort of man who might be found in this forest. Certainly no one would suspect a man looking like Blade, tramping along with an ax over his shoulder, of being from a world far beyond the imagination of anyone in this Dimension.

He couldn't have found himself a better disguise if he'd thought the matter over for a solid week. The computer had done its usual job of altering his brain so that he both spoke and understood the local language, so he'd have no problems there. He could move on at his own pace, going where he wanted, listening and learning without attracting any notice.

That would be more than useful. It could save his life. Blade suspected that sooner or later rumors of wandering strangers in this Dimension reached the wolf's-head riders or their master. He didn't want them coming after him before he knew more about them.

Blade still did not have quite enough faith in his disguise to head openly down the road. He kept under cover of the trees, just within sight of the road, as long as the forest lasted. Once he saw a civilian rider pass, spurring his shaggy mount to a ponderous gallop. Another time he saw a cart loaded with clattering barrels rumble past behind four yoked oxen.

After three hours Blade was out of the forest and into cultivated land again. Here there were orchards instead of vineyards, row after row of squat close-grown trees with blackish green leaves and small blue flowers that exhaled an overpowering sweetness. Men and women were already busily at work among the trees with knives, hooks, and binding ropes, or on the stone walls that separated the orchards.

Each party of workers greeted Blade as they saw him, dropped their tools, and crowded around him. In a medieval world of isolated villages, any stranger could earn a welcome by bringing news.

"We heard that the Wolves came down on Frinda," said one man. "Did you hear or see anything of it?"

Frinda must be the village Blade had seen raided, and the Wolves could only be the armored riders. He shook his head, hoping in that way to learn more from these people. "No. They had no work for me, so I passed on through. I must have been in the forest before the Wolves came to Frinda, and yesterday was not a time to see far."

The man nodded. "Perhaps it's a good thing you didn't stay. You'd have stood great good chance of the Wolves taking you. Strong, young, healthy, wandering with no kin to miss you and mutter—aye, the Wolves like such as you."

"So I've heard," said Blade cautiously. "What of your village, my friend? I'll work for you with pleasure, but if the Wolves are going to come down on you like they did on Frinda—"

"Na, na," the man said, shaking his head. "We of Isstano are not those of Frinda. We'd not shelter a Chosen Girl like those fools did. They brought the Wolves on themselves, they did. We know better."

So the Wolves collected tribute or taxes for their unknown master and punished those who tried to evade their share. That didn't surprise Blade. What did surprise him was the way those peasants spoke of the Wolves. They seemed to be proud of being dutiful and obedient, with no thought of resisting the Wolves, any more than of resisting the weather or the passage of the seasons. Something had driven all thought of rebellion out of their minds. Was it the skill in arms of the Wolves, or perhaps something more? Blade wondered.

He listened carefully to the gossip in the village that afternoon as he chopped firewood, split rails for fences, and cut beams for a cattle shed. What he heard confirmed his first impressions. This Dimension—or at least this land of Rentoro—was ruled with an iron hand by some powerful tyrant. The Wolves on their shaggy white heudas were the tyrant's army and police. They enforced his laws, collected his taxes and his slaves, and suppressed any signs of rebellion against his authority. A Chosen Girl was one the tyrant had picked out, no doubt for his harem. The one who'd fled to the village of Frinda instead of meekly accepting her fate had committed an act of rebellion. By sheltering her, even out of pure kindness, the village of Frinda joined her in that rebellion. To be sure, it was only a small act of rebellion, so the punishment was light. The tyrant seldom turned the Wolves loose to kill, destroy, and burn indiscriminately.

That made a grim sort of sense. The tyrant appeared to see everything and everyone in Rentoro as his personal property. A wise man, no matter how brutal he might be, did not wantonly destroy his own property. This tyrant was wise—the careful training he'd given his Wolves showed that clearly enough.

The Wolves had their training and their armor, while the people of Rentoro seemed to have nothing but axes, light hunting bows, and boar spears. So half a dozen Wolves could do as they pleased in a village. A hundred could no doubt do the same in a town.

Blade learned a good deal about the Wolves from listening to village gossip, but not much about their master. In fact, he didn't even learn the man's name or title. Neither was ever mentioned. The villagers seldom mentioned the tyrant at all, and when they did they referred to him solemnly as "he."

Blade was frustrated and annoyed, although he was also sorry for the villagers. Asking them to violate what seemed to be a rigid taboo would simply frighten them. That would cost Blade his chance of a hot meal and a warm bed in the village tonight, and perhaps more. The villagers talked of the tyrant as if he knew everything that went on in Rentoro. This suggested a large force of loyal spies. Suspicious questions might lead Blade not to information but to a lonely grave.

So he kept his mouth shut, ate the bread and meat the village headman offered him, and slept comfortably in the straw of a barn. In the morning he ate more bread, drank warm milk fresh from the cow, accepted a bundle of sausage, and moved on.

Blade was on the move for the next six days, from village to village and from farm to farm. He drifted north, then east, then back toward the south, guiding himself by the sun and by the peasants' advice. In each village and at each farm he was able to exchange a few hours' work with his ax for a bed and a meal. Once they threw in a handful of crude brass coins.

No one seemed to suspect that Blade was anything other than what he seemed to be—a traveling woodcutter and carpenter. No one hesitated about talking freely in his presence. No one told him anything he hadn't learned in the first village. After the first couple of days he more or less gave up expecting to hear anything new.

Rentoro was a rich and fertile land, the people well-fed, the animals sleek, the houses snug and clean. Apart from the Wolves, the tyrant's hand did not seem to fall heavily on his people. In this land of fertile soil and hard-working peasants, a wise ruler could certainly collect all the wealth he wanted without leaving anyone hungry or homeless.

Blade's six days of travel were one of the most pleasant vacations he'd ever had. He had plenty of food, fresh air, and exercise, and very little to guard against or worry about. He knew he could quite cheerfully wander about Rentoro this way for another month.

One of these days, if he went on traveling into Dimension X, he would probably have to do just that. One of these days he would find a Dimension with no technology, no great empires, no wars to fight, and no resources or secrets to be dug out and brought back to Home Dimension. Then there would be nothing for him to do but find a place to live and a way to make a living until it was time to return to Home Dimension. He'd have to thank Lord Leighton for the excellent vacation when this happened.

It wasn't going to happen in this Dimension, though. There was no sign of the Wolves during Blade's days on the road, but they were never entirely out of his mind. The Wolves and the mysterious tyrant who sent them out were a mystery. Behind every mystery Blade had ever found in Dimension X lay something dangerous, and also something valuable.

Chapter 5

On the evening of the sixth day Blade reached a farm lying at the foot of a range of wooded hills. Over dinner in the farmer's hut Blade learned that beyond the hills lay a walled town called Dodini. There was no good wagon road over the hills, so the farmers on this side did little trading with the town. But a strong man on his own two feet could easily pass through the forest up to the crest of the range.

"Then ye be seein' town for yeself, and a good mornin's walk'll take ye there."

A town large enough to need walls and impress these peasants might have only a few thousand people. It still sounded more like civilization than anything Blade had seen so far in Rentoro. It was time to bring his vacation to an end.

Blade left the farm well before dawn the next morning, not sure exactly how far he had to travel but hoping to reach Dodini before dark. He plunged into the forest as the sky turned light. Fortunately it was a clear day, and the canopy of branches overhead was thin enough so he could guide himself by the sun. Within an hour the trees were growing thinner, and an hour later he was striding across open moorland. The grass was long enough to ripple pleasantly in the stiff breeze, and bushes studded with pale red flowers seemed to be everywhere.

Shortly before noon he reached the crest of the range and saw the country beyond spread out before him. Through it ran a large river, so blue that it seemed to glow in the sunlight, and on the banks of the river squatted a walled town. Both walls and town seemed to sprout towers everywhere and smoke curled up from many chimneys. Blade measured the distance and heaved a sigh of relief. The town was less than ten miles away. He shifted the ax to the other shoulder and started downhill.

Blade reached level ground in an hour and in two more he

was halfway to Dodini. A few hundred yards ahead the path he was following joined a wide road, roughly paved with stone slabs. To the right of the path rose a rock hill, its slopes too bare and steep to support even grass. Blade headed for this hill. It would give him a final chance to examine the town from a safely concealed perch, before entering it.

He reached the hill and scrambled up the near side. The bare rock reflected the heat of the sun until the slope was like a griddle. Blade's clothes were dark with sweat and torn in several places long before he reached the top of the hill.

He was only a few yards below the top when he heard a sudden soft *thump* that seemed to come from the other side of the hill. It sounded like an enormous feather mattress falling. Blade froze, then heard a more familiar sound—iron-shod hooves, moving fast across a hard surface. Blade flung himself toward the hilltop. As he reached it, the sound of human shouts joined the clatter of hooves. He threw himself flat and stared down the far slope of the hill.

The Wolves had come to Dodini. At least forty of them were heading down the hill, their heudas kicking up clouds of dust and gravel. Blade counted seven of the fully armored leaders with their shields and pennoned lances, with a cluster of men-at-arms following each one.

At least half the men-at-arms were leading pack heudas with large leather sacks or wicker baskets slung on either side. The heudas were ungraceful, almost grotesque in their movements, but they covered ground at a pace no horse could have matched on that slope.

Blade's eyes followed the trail of dust across the hillside to a pair of large boulders, each twice as high as a man. With a sudden shock he realized that the trail ended there. All the Wolves seemed to be riding out of the gap between the boulders—but none of them rode into a gap from the other side. The rising cloud of dust did not conceal the hillside beyond the boulders. It lay bare, empty, and undisturbed.

Blade looked again, more carefully, and saw the same thing he'd seen the first time. He forced himself to consider what it meant. He might be hallucinating. His eyes might be playing perfectly normal tricks on him—overlooking some natural feature which hid the Wolves until they appeared between the boulders.

Or he might be seeing what was actually happening—the

24

Wolves appearing out of thin air and riding off toward Dodini.

Blade refused to use the word "impossible." It was always foolish, and in Dimension X it was dangerous. Still, a force of heavy cavalry riding out of thin air wasn't something he met every day, even in Dimension X.

Suddenly the mystery behind the Wolves was much greater than before. The secret behind the Wolves was no longer just the identity of their master. It was much more—how much more Blade didn't even want to try guessing for now. For now that would be a waste of time.

The vacation was definitely over, though.

Blade lay on his stomach until the last of the Wolves appeared and rode off down the hill. Among the men-at-arms behind the last leader Blade recognized the huge red-bearded man who'd wielded the ax in Frinda.

There were more than a hundred Wolves in sight by the time they stopped coming. As the last ones thundered off down the hill, the first ones were already reaching level ground. They spurred their mounts toward the road that led to Dodini. Farmers in the fields scampered out of the Wolves' path or threw themselves to the ground.

The Wolves struck the road, swung to the left, and pounded off toward Dodini. A thin column of red smoke seemed to be curling up from one of the towers. Otherwise the town lay quiet in the sunlight, as if the Wolves charging at its walls were no more than a thunderstorm which would come and go regardless of what men did.

As the last Wolf struck the road, Blade sprang up and scrambled down the hillside as fast as he could. On level ground he broke into a run. He headed straight for the town, cutting across fields and through woods, feet pounding, long legs eating up the ground. He could hardly have run faster if the Wolves had been behind him rather than ahead of him.

If he could get his hands on one of the Wolves, things would be a great deal simpler. But to do that safely he had to reach Dodini hard on the Wolves' heels. In the uproar of their arrival, no one would be paying attention to a ragged stranger with an ax over his shoulder.

There were many things that could go wrong with this rough plan. There always were, when one man decided to challenge a hundred. Meanwhile, there was nothing to do but run. Blade ran, and ahead of him the towers of Dodini rose higher and higher above the trees.

A final patch of woods gave Blade cover almost up to the walls. The trees grew so close that Blade wondered if the people of Dodini had ever heard of enemies creeping up to their walls under this ready cover. Had Dodini been at peace, except for the Wolves, since before these trees were planted? That was a long time. The trees were solid gray-barked things two feet thick at the base. They might have been here for a century or more.

This suggested not just one tyrant, keeping the peace in this Dimension by sending out the Wolves to collect his taxes and crush his enemies. It suggested a whole dynasty of tyrants, extending back a century or more, tightening their rule, picking and training their troops, getting people to accept their authority as something inevitable and inescapable, ruthlessly enforcing peace. Now Richard Blade faced that dynasty single-handed, ready to challenge its picked troops and try to dig out its secret—or die trying.

It was not going to be the easiest challenge he'd ever met. However, he'd faced longer odds in other Dimensions. He was still alive and most of the people who'd tried to kill him were dead. He'd just have to go ahead once more, do his best, and trust to luck for what he couldn't control. So far luck had been with him, and his best had been very good indeed.

It might even be good enough to keep him alive against a hundred Wolves.

Chapter 6

Blade crept to the edge of the trees and peered out. Luck was going to be with him, at least for now. Only two Wolves guarded the nearest gate into Dodini, and only one of them was mounted. The one on foot stood with his back to Blade, eyes firmly fixed on the narrow street visible through the gateway. The mounted Wolf sat with his heuda's head toward the trees. He himself spent half his time looking back over his shoulder into the town, rather than toward the trees or along the narrow road at the base of the wall on either side of him.

Blade was not entirely surprised to find only two Wolves. A hundred Wolves might seem like a mighty army, but in fact they would be spread fairly thin against a town the size of Dodini. Simply keeping the streets clear could use up fifty men. Two men at each gate would be enough to keep any hotheads from trying to lock the Wolves into Dodini and give warning of anyone trying to escape.

Nor was it surprising that the two Wolves were not completely alert. They were well-trained and well-disciplined, but they were also men who expected little resistance and no real fighting. Perhaps they were like the legions of Rome—men whose fathers and grandfathers had carried all before them, until they could no longer believe that anyone in the world would even try to stand against the Wolves. They were about to get a rude surprise.

Blade was happy to find Wolves at the gates. He wouldn't have to enter Dodini, hunt down a Wolf through its streets, then bring the man safely out again. He could strike at the men here, then have weapons, a heuda, a prisoner to question, and nothing else to do except get away from Dodini as fast as possible. He could only hope that his blow against the Wolves wouldn't bring some bloody retaliation against the town.

Blade's eyes scanned a half-circle from right to left, taking in everything along the edge of the trees, the road, and the wall of Dodini. The wall curved so that the other gates and their guards were out of sight. They wouldn't be out of hearing, though. He'd have to move fast. Fortunately the ground between Blade and the road was clear and level. A ditch lay on the far side of the road, between it and the wall, shallow and filled with scummy water, but that would be more of a problem for the two Wolves than for Blade. He moved a few yards to the right, gripped his ax, and got ready to charge.

He was about to leap to his feet when he heard a distant but unmistakable roll of thunder. As it died away he heard the echoing rattle of hooves on stone approaching along the street inside the gate. A Wolf appeared, mace swinging in one hand and leading his heuda with the other. Across the animal's back was tied a slender young woman with long dark hair, wearing only a stained and ragged shift.

As the Wolf stepped out of the shadows Blade recognized the red-bearded axman of Frinda. He led his mount out through the gate, across the wooden bridge over the ditch, and onto the road. Then he looped the reins negligently over a bush and drew his knife to cut the woman's bindings.

The mounted Wolf looked at him, and a grin spread across his face. "Ho, Sigo, you dog, you! I never thought I'd see you snatch off one of his Chosen. Are you ready to kiss your balls good-bye, then? I'd hardly thought you'd done all you wanted with them, but—"

"Oh, hold your wind, Ketz," said the red-bearded Sigo. He hacked through the bindings of the woman's wrists and stepped around to do the same at her ankles. "This is no Chosen, for I'm no fool. These sheep in Dodini aren't going to do anything we need fear, so I thought I'd snatch one of their ewes for a bit of our own pleasure." He freed the woman's ankles, grabbed her by one leg and one arm, and heaved her over his shoulder.

"Besides, I'm really doing her a favor," Sigo went on, as he carried the woman across the road. "After we're through with her, she can no longer be a Chosen. I don't imagine you mind the trade, do you, little one? A few minutes with us, instead of a lifetime serving *him*?" He slung the woman off his shoulder and dropped her with a thud in the grass. If she said anything, Blade couldn't hear it. She lay motionless while Sigo began unlacing his trousers.

"Now then," he said. "You'd better be a little more lively now, or it won't be just a few minutes with us. I'm not going to have my fun with—*hayaiiiii!*" he screamed, as Blade sprang out into the open.

Sigo had left his mace and crossbow with his heuda and was unarmed except for his knife. Blade closed in, Sigo threw up his free hand and thrust with the knife in the other. Blade's ax hissed down in a precise arc and Sigo's raised hand flew from its wrist. Sigo cried out again, but did not miss a step as he came at Blade, the dagger held with the grip of a trained knife fighter, ready for an upward thrust.

Sigo closed so fast that he got inside Blade's guard. Blade leaped backward as the dagger thrust up at his stomach. At the same time he raised the ax and smashed the five-foot handle across Sigo's neck. The dagger's edge tore Blade's trousers and the point pricked his skin. The impact of the ax handle knocked Sigo off his feet. He sprawled on his back, still clutching the dagger, trying to raise both his good hand and his bloody stump to ward off Blade. He was still trying when Blade brought the ax down on his chest. Sigo doubled up in one final convulsive spasm and gasped, "The Wizard will avenge me." Then he fell back, limp and dead.

While Blade and Sigo fought, the mounted Wolf was unslinging and cocking his crossbow. He didn't dare fire, though, for fear of hitting his comrade. As Blade stepped back from Sigo's body, the archer found himself with a clear target. The crossbow came up, and as it did the woman suddenly came to life. She leaped to her feet, then lunged for Sigo's fallen dagger.

The movement drew the archer's eye as his finger closed on the trigger of the crossbow. The bolt that should have left Blade as dead as Sigo whistled harmlessly across the road and sank into a tree. Before either the woman or the archer could make another move, Blade charged across the road, ax held high and ready to strike.

The archer spurred his heuda into motion. It lurched forward, two, three, four slow steps. Then the Wolf dug in his spurs again, the massive hind legs quivered and tensed, and Blade swung sharply to the left. As the Wolf charged past him, he shifted his grip on the ax and swung it in a wide arc, his arms stretched out as far as they would go.

He struck with the blunt side of the ax head, in case he missed his mark and struck the heuda instead of the man.

The last thing he wanted to do was kill or even wound the animal. It was the safest way out of here, for him, for his prisoner, and now for the young woman.

Blade's ax smashed into the Wolf's side, hard enough to knock the wind out of him. His hands clutched the reins, pulling the heuda to a stop. The animal reared, pawing the air, then started to turn toward Blade. Blade shifted sideways, to keep away from the head with its jutting horns. Then he struck again, as the man drew his sword and raised it for a downward cut. The ax smashed the Wolf's sword aside and bit through his helmet as if it was a tin can. His eyes went blank, blood gushed from mouth and ears, and he toppled out of the saddle.

"Behind you!" the woman screamed. "Behind you! Behind—!" as thunder crashed overhead. Blade didn't need to have the words repeated even once. He was already whirling, ax ready, as the last Wolf charged at him from the gate. Blade raised the ax, the Wolf's sword whirled toward him, and its edge bit into the ax handle. The steel went halfway through the wood at one blow and stuck. Blade heaved on the ax, jerking the man toward him. The Wolf kept his grip on the sword and let Blade pull him in, then suddenly let go and leaped on Blade with his bare hands. Both fighters went down from the impact.

Blade found himself grappling the Wolf on the ground as if the man really was a wild animal. The man was smaller than Blade, but strong, nearly as fast, and utterly desperate. He bit, he clawed, he tried to gouge and tear every part of Blade's body he could reach, he shouted and screamed like a madman. Blade was too busy keeping his eyes and testicles from being mangled to try anything scientific against the Wolf. It was a straight contest of brute strength and ferocity.

The two men rolled over and over as they fought. Blade was vaguely aware of thunder rolling louder and more often from a darkening sky. He was more aware of the woman standing in the road, dagger in her hand, staring at the two fighters. He hoped that if she tried to join the fight she'd get the dagger into the Wolf, not into him!

Then suddenly Blade felt the ground dropping away under him. He barely had time to take a deep breath before he and the Wolf plunged into the scum-coated water of the ditch along the wall.

Blade had his lungs filled and his mouth closed as he went

under. The Wolf didn't. He sucked in a great lungful of filthy water and exploded to the surface, coughing and choking horribly, clawing at his throat. Blade rose up beside him and slammed the heel of one hand up under the man's jaw. The Wolf sprawled backward against the bank with his head and shoulders out of the water. Before he could clear his lungs, Blade gripped his throat with both hands and squeezed hard. The Wolf's windpipe collapsed and his eyes rolled wildly. He wriggled and twisted like a worm on a hook for a moment, then finally lay still.

Blade scrambled up on to the bank and looked around. The heuda was snorting, honking, pawing the ground, and weaving its head from side to side. Blade picked up one of the Wolves' helmets and walked toward the animal, making soothing noises. The thunder overhead was growing louder and more frequent, but in the intervals between the crashes and rumbles Blade could hear horns and drums sounding inside Dodini. The alarm was up.

The woman was standing beside the heuda. Her garment showed several new stains and rips. Her face showed fear, relief, surprise, and disbelief all at once. She was shaking slightly, but the long-fingered hands she held out in front of her were steady. Good. If she hadn't panicked yet, she probably wouldn't.

Blade reached the heuda, stroked its neck, and patted its muzzle, until the animal stood quietly. Then he tied the ax to the saddle and swung himself up into it. He reached a hand down toward the woman.

"Come with me," he said. "We must leave Dodini, or the Wolves will be upon us." He hoped she'd trust him enough to come with him. The three Wolves were all dead, so he'd have no prisoner to tell him about "the Wizard." The woman might not know as much as the Wolves, but she'd know more than he did at the moment.

The woman stared at Blade, eyes wide and nose wrinkling up. He didn't blame her for either. He must be an appalling sight, a giant of a man in a dented helmet and clothes that looked like a ragpicker's, armed to the teeth, coated with blood and the foul-smelling muck of the ditch.

The woman stared for a moment longer, then gripped Blade's hand and let him swing her up into the saddle behind him. Blade dug his heels into the heuda's side and pulled its head around. It reared, then leaped forward and galloped

31

away down the road. The gate and the sprawled bodies disappeared around the curve of the wall of Dodini. From high above a crossbow sent a bolt whistling past them. Then the thunder exploded overhead with a sound like the heavens falling and the world was blotted out by a gray curtain of rain.

Chapter 7

Blade didn't know how far a heuda could carry two people at a full gallop. He did know he was probably going to find out before this day was over.

At least they had the storm and that was a blessing. As long as it lasted, they would be nearly invisible and their trail would be wiped out almost as fast as they left it. Besides, the Wolves might be good fighters, but Blade wondered if they'd be good at tracking across country. They might have little need for the skill and less chance to practice, if all their victims waited quietly for them like turkeys in a pen.

For a few minutes the rain was coming down so hard that Blade had to slow the heuda to a walk. It was impossible to see the road more than ten feet ahead and he didn't want to ride straight into a ditch or a storm-swollen stream. Even at a walk it took all Blade's attention to keep the heuda on the road.

Once or twice he had a chance to look more closely at the woman behind him. She rode in silence, her arms locked about his waist, her long graceful legs gripping the heuda tightly. Her sodden hair hung down in strings over shoulders and face and her shift was molded to her body. She was slim, but by no means unattractive. Her face was now a blank mask, the mask of someone shutting out the world while she tried to understand what was happening to her.

After twenty minutes the rain slackened off enough so that Blade could safely urge the heuda to a gallop. They pounded down the stone-paved road leading out of Dodini, splashing through puddles in a cloud of spray. Fields and pastures and an occasional hut showed on either side of the road. There was no one to see them pass, not with the Wolves out and the storm overhead.

They thundered across a wooden bridge over a small river turned swollen and ugly by the storm. A mile beyond the bridge the paved road ended. Now Blade began to wonder if the storm was such a complete blessing. The dirt road ahead was rapidly turning into mud and in places into a pond. He kept the heuda moving as fast as it could go, and the mud splashed up to coat both mount and riders until they looked like statues.

Gradually the land rose under them. The road began to swing back and forth as it climbed a long hillside, the earth underfoot turned from black to sandy brown, and the going became easier. At the same time the rain slackened still more. In spite of his superb senses of direction, Blade now had only a very vague idea of which way they'd come from Dodini. He hoped the Wolves had even less idea of which way their prey had gone.

On the crest of the hill Blade turned the heuda off the road and reined in under cover of the trees. Then he dismounted and examined the animal. It was breathing heavily, but looked good for quite a few more miles. The gear he'd captured with the heuda, on the other hand, was disappointing.

There was a spare dagger and a sharpening stone. There was a rusty awl and some leather thongs for repairing harness. There was enough food for a light meal—dried fruit, strong-smelling cheese, salt meat the color and toughness of wood. A leather bottle on the saddle held about a quart of sour wine. The only real surprise was a package, wrapped in dark red silk, that Blade found lurking in the very bottom of the sack. Unwrapped, it turned out to be a necklace of heavy metal bars linked by enameled silver hooks. Judging from the weight of the necklace, the metal bars were solid gold.

Over the next few days, that necklace might be quite useful, but not right now. They needed more food and also some dry clothing for the woman, who had nothing but her sodden shift between her and the weather. Blade could feel her shivering.

They'd have to raid a farm or a village for what they needed. That would mean revealing themselves to people who could remember them and tell tales to pursuing Wolves. It was a risk, but one they'd have to take. It was also one that could be greatly reduced with a little careful planning. Blade climbed into the saddle again and started the heuda off at a walk. Then he turned back to look at the woman. Her eyes met his and she managed a faint smile.

"What is your name?" he asked.

"Lorya," she replied.

"Lorya, we need to get some food and clothing. So when we see another village, we will leave the road and ride around it through the fields and forests. That way no one will see us. Then I will leave you in the forest on the far side of the village and ride back to get the food and clothing from the people."

Fear showed in Lorya's eyes at the idea of being left alone in unknown country so far from Dodini. Blade gently patted her shoulder. She stiffened, then slowly relaxed and again smiled faintly.

"Do not worry. I will not abandon you. I will return as quickly as I can, and I will leave you the other knife and the food in case something happens to me. I do not think it will, though. How often do the people in the villages try to fight his Wolves, even one of them riding alone?"

Lorya's smile vanished and she said in a level voice, "They do not do it. Not if they are wise." Her tone suggested that she took no pleasure in the Wizard's rule, but had no idea it could ever be challenged or resisted. For the twentieth time, Blade wondered what the Wizard had beside the Wolves to make people regard him as invincible.

Blade turned his attention back to the road. Showers of rain came and went, but the sky remained thickly overcast. Where trees shaded the road, they left it in a murky twilight. Blade rode out of one of those stretches of twilight to find himself on the rim of a wooded valley. At the bottom of the valley a village sprawled among a tangle of fields and orchards.

Blade swung wide of the village, picking his way down the side of the valley to the stream that flowed along the bottom. He crossed the stream a mile below the village, the foaming brown water rising as high as his stirrups. Then he rode up the other side of the valley, keeping under cover of the trees as much as possible.

At last he reached a good hiding place on the trail that led down the hill toward the village. He reined in, and without a word Lorya slipped out of the saddle. He handed her the food, the dagger, and the ax. After a moment's thought he also gave her the necklace. He'd considered taking at least a couple of the bars down to the village and leaving them, but that would not be wise. The dead Wolf's comrades might recognize the gold, and besides, the Wolves never seemed to

35

pay for anything. If he wanted to be taken for a Wolf, he would have to be as greedy and brutal as one, as uncomfortable as the idea was.

Lorya gaped at the necklace and tried to hand it back. Blade shook his head. "Keep it. I won't need it in the village. If I don't come back, you will. You can sell the bars one at a time. I imagine you can find buyers?"

"Yes."

Blade wasn't surprised. The people of Rentoro might be peaceful under the rule of the Wizard and his Wolves, but they were men, not angels. There would be thieves and there would be receivers for what the thieves stole. There was enough gold in that necklace to take Lorya a long way.

She reached up, squeezed Blade's hand in farewell, and disappeared into the trees. Blade tied the red silk over his face, hiding everything but his eyes. Then he urged the heuda down the trail toward the village at a brisk trot.

His plan was simple. The Wolves might have no idea of who or what they were looking for, since the only three who'd got a good look at him were dead. If by some chance they did know, they would be looking for a man with an ax and a woman, riding double on a war heuda.

Either way, they would not get much help from the people of the village. The villagers would see only a single man, face masked, without an ax, riding a heuda so splashed with mud that no markings would be visible. They could describe this man until they were blue in the face, without making the hunt for Blade and Lorya much easier.

It was not a perfect plan, but it was by far the best Blade could manage with what he had. It would have to do.

The trail grew steadily wider, although it still sloped sharply downward. Blade urged the heuda up to a canter. Not for the first time, he was glad to be riding a heuda instead of a horse. A heuda could trot or canter on slopes where a horse would have to walk or risk breaking a leg.

As Blade rode out of the trees, the ground leveled out. Five hundred yards straight ahead lay the village. Blade urged the heuda up to a gallop and he was in the main street of the village, shouting war cries from half a dozen different Dimensions, before anyone there could react. He jerked the heuda to a stop so violently that it reared up on its hind legs in a spatter of mud.

"Ho!" he shouted. The silk mask over his face distorted his

voice, but the sheer volume made everyone whirl to stare at him. He drew his sword and pointed it at the nearest grown man.

"You! I pass on the business of the Wizard!" The man started and swallowed hard at the mention of the forbidden name. "I need food, wine, and dry clothing. Bring it, and make haste or face the Wizard's wrath!"

The dozen people in the street scattered. They could not have run much faster if Blade had opened up on them with a machine gun. They were back within minutes, carrying armfuls of bread, cheese, and dried meat, skins of wine and beer, and enough clothing for a dozen men. Blade ordered them to put what they'd brought into sacks and tie the sacks to his saddle. He sat on his heuda as they worked, arms crossed on his chest, playing as well as he could the role of a master being waited on by his servants. His eyes never stopped scanning the street, though, and his hand never went far from the hilt of his sword. One Wolf, riding alone, might be too much of a temptation for some brave fool. That would be a disaster for everybody, starting with Blade himself.

Eventually sacks hung from Blade's saddle like ripe grapes. He brandished his sword in the air and the people scattered from around the heuda. Blade turned his mount and cantered back up the street, wishing he had eyes in the back of his head and half-expecting every moment to hear the whistle of an arrow. Damn it, there must be *something* these people would not endure from the Wizard or his Wolves!

He was clear of the village within minutes. He let the heuda climb the trail at a walk, for it was panting and sweat was making trails in the mud on its flanks. Finally he reached the place where he'd left Lorya. As silently as a forest spirit she came out of the trees and climbed up behind him, holding the ax across her lap.

They rode on for the rest of the afternoon and finally stopped deep in a stretch of virgin forest as it began to grow dark. Blade guessed they must have come a good twenty miles from Dodini and were about as safe as they could hope to be. Until the Wolves in Dodini knew which way the fugitives had gone, they'd be facing the job of searching an area the size of an English county. A hundred men couldn't do it. A thousand might, but it would take time to gather a thousand Wolves. In that time Blade and Lorya would be traveling on as fast as they could. Meanwhile, the Wolves gathering to search for them could not collect taxes and slaves or rape women elsewhere in Rentoro. By simply staying alive and on the move, Blade and Lorya would be interfering with the Wizard's ability to rule the land of Rentoro.

Unless the Wizard decided to ignore them completely? That didn't seem likely. The Wizard's power depended on the Wolves, and the Wolves' power depended on their ability to crush any rebellion the moment it reared its head. If those who'd slain three Wolves were allowed to go unpunished, who knew what might happen? One unpunished rebellion could inspire a dozen others—and there could be only so many of the Wolves.

No, he and Lorya would have the Wizard and the Wolves on their trail for a long time—perhaps as long as he was in this Dimension. Learning more about the Wizard was no longer just a matter of discovering his secrets—it was a matter of life and death.

With dry pith from the heart of a dead tree and flint and steel from the village, Blade was able to start a small fire. He dried kindling, then step by step built up the fire until it was blazing merrily. He pulled off his own clothes and hung them over branches stuck in the ground by the fire. Lorya took some of the clothes from the village and modestly retired behind a tree to pull them on. Then she hung her sodden shift over the branch and huddled as close to the fire as she dared while Blade prepared dinner.

They ate smoked meat, cheese, loaves of flat dark bread, and washed it all down with wine. The wine was raw, but it warmed them from inside as the fire warmed them from outside. When they'd eaten all they could, Blade wrapped a blanket around Lorya and put an arm across her shoulders in a brotherly fashion.

"Now, Lorya," he said. "I have traveled to Rentoro from a distant land. I have been here for more than a week, and I still do not understand much of what I have seen. Indeed, I have seen nothing like the Wolves in any of the lands I have visited. Tell me about the Wolves and about the Wizard who is their master."

Lorya shivered at hearing the name of the Wizard from Blade's lips. He tightened his arm around her and gently drew her head down on to his shoulder. "No, Lorya. I will not believe that the Wizard can punish us for saying his name."

38

"You must believe it," she said. "You must. He can. I know it."

"You will have to tell me more," said Blade. "How can the Wizard do this?"

"It is easy, when you are—" she hesitated.

"The Wizard," said Blade firmly. "Get used to calling him by his proper name, and perhaps he will not seem so terrible."

"That cannot be," said Lorya. "He always has been terrible and always will be. By magic he sees all that happens in Rentoro, and by magic he sends the Wolves to punish his enemies. It has been so since my great-grandfather's time, and it will always be so."

"Now it is my turn to say 'That cannot be,'" said Blade with a smile. "The Wizard of Rentoro sounds even stranger than his Wolves. Tell me about him." His voice was low, but he used the brisk, firm tone of a man who would not argue any further.

So Lorya told him about the Wizard of Rentoro.

Chapter 8

The Wizard came to Rentoro a century ago, she told him. No one knew where he came from, then or now. For all that anyone could tell, he might have fallen from the sky, and indeed there were some in Rentoro who believed that he had done so. Certainly it was hard to believe that any man born of woman on this earth could do all the things the Wizard of Rentoro had done in his hundred years of rule.

The first thing he did was call all the men and women of the nearest town to come forth to him. Some came of their own free will, because they were curious. Others at first refused to come, out of fear of a man they believed to be an evil sorcerer. Those who refused to come heard a voice in their minds—a voice that spoke without any words, but one which commanded them to come forth and meet the Wizard. At last even the bravest and strongest could no longer resist the commands in their minds.

So a whole town came forth and the Wizard put them to work. They built him a castle like none ever seen before in Rentoro, with four round towers as tall as great trees and walls so thick men could ride on heudas along their tops. They built houses all around the castle, and then another wall outside the houses. They built still more walls, running in all directions and meeting each other at odd angles. This caused some to say that the Wizard was mad. Finally they built another wall outside everything else, with huge gates in it.

Most of the children of the town died of hunger while their parents worked to build the Wizard's castle. Many of the men also died. Some died from too much work. Others were simply found dead in their tents in the morning. It was said that men who talked of escaping were particularly likely to be found dead in this way. Some of the women also died, and many were called to serve the lust of the Wizard or of those men he had found to serve him.

40

Not everyone hated the Wizard or saw him as an enemy. There were those who saw him as a powerful friend, whose magical powers might do much for those who served him freely. Most of these were men without masters, trades, or homes, rough strong men with little but their swords, the clothes they wore, and the heudas they rode. Many of these came to offer their services to the Wizard. He accepted them and made them into his Wolves.

He taught them to use weapons never seen before in Rentoro, such as the crossbows that could shoot bolts through oak doors. He taught them to make and wear the armor of steel plates and steel rings that few weapons in Rentoro could pierce. He divided them into bands of seven, each with a leader who wore armor all over and six who followed him, all seven mounted on fine, strong heudas.

The Wolves served the Wizard faithfully. He spoke to the leaders in the voice that had no words, giving them their orders. They in turn passed on the orders to those who followed them. The bands of Wolves swept all before them.

It took a generation and a few years more, but at the end of that time the Wizard ruled in Rentoro. Many fought against his rule and most of them died. They outnumbered the Wolves, to be sure, and after the first ten years they had weapons as good as the Wolves'. In a fair fight, the men of Rentoro might have beaten the Wolves.

But there had never been a fair fight, and there never would be, not against the Wizard's Wolves. The Wizard's magic fought on their side, and so no man could beat them.

"How does the Wizard's magic fight for them?" was Blade's question at this point.

Lorya could only tell Blade what she'd heard, and even about that she was vague. It took some time for Blade to understand what the Wizard's magic did—or at least seemed to do.

First, the Wizard saw everything that happened in Rentoro. At least he saw everything that went on in any city or town. Sooner or later, he also learned everything that happened in any village or farm that might be the smallest danger to his rule.

Whenever there was any such danger, the Wolves struck with their swift swords and bows. Men, women, and children died, many of them in particularly horrible ways. No one

41

who survived could ever forget what he'd seen happen to those who defied the Wizard.

The Wolves rode into battle on their fine heudas, but they did not ride about Rentoro on them. The Wizard's magic sent them from place to place, faster even than a bird could fly through the air. This was certain, for the same Wolves had been seen fighting on the same day, in two towns more than a week's ride apart. This had happened not just once but many times.

So no army could assemble to fight the Wizard without his quickly learning of it. Indeed, it was dangerous to even talk of assembling such an army. Long before the rebels could be ready, the Wolves always came down upon them. No matter how many men the rebels might hope to have, when the battle was joined the Wolves always had more. So the Wolves always won, and then the survivors of the rebel army were burned or impaled or flogged to death, saw their wives raped, heard their children scream as they were thrown off walls.

It did not take many such battles and the butchery that came after them to drive home the lesson. Soon the Wizard had few enemies, and many men and women in the cities and towns who served him. Some served him out of fear, some out of hope of reward, some to be avenged on enemies. A few saw his rule as a good thing for Rentoro. In time the Wizard had so many servants he hardly needed his magic to tell him what was happening in Rentoro. In any city or town he had a hundred pairs of eyes to watch his enemies and a hundred pairs of lips to tell him what they might be planning. Sometimes he even had men willing to take up their own swords for him, so that the Wolves were not needed.

Although rebels were now few, the Wolves still had plenty of work. The Wizard's castle had as many people in it as a small city. It needed food and wine, firewood and iron, wagons and harness, heudas and draft animals, and much else. The Wolves regularly gathered all these things throughout Rentoro.

They also gathered an annual tax, paid in gold, silver, and jewels, silk and fine weapons, young women and young men. The young women were always beautiful and everyone understood why the Wizard wanted them. The men were always the strongest and healthiest to be found, and it was less certain why the Wizard needed them. Certainly even his vast castle could not need so many servants and laborers? In any case, neither the men nor the women were ever seen again after the Wolves took them away.

This was the life the people of Rentoro had now led for three generations, since the last rebels were crushed outside the walls of the city of Morina. It was not the best life imaginable, but it was far from unbearable. The Wizard's taxes were never more than a man or a town could easily pay, and the Wolves seldom stole anything or hurt anyone without the Wizard's orders. Of course, if one was a strong young man or a beautiful young woman, an unknown fate was always hanging over one's head. Even that was something people could come to endure, given time.

Lorya herself was twenty, the daughter of a stablekeeper. She'd made a good marriage at eighteen, to the son and heir of a master harness maker. At nineteen she was a widow, for the Wolves came and took her husband away, leaving her with a child three months old. Four months after that, the child was dead of a fever. So being raped by the Wolves did not seem to her a great deal worse than what had already happened to her. She'd been quite ready to endure it as best she could when Blade came on the scene, as unexpected and as deadly as a thunderbolt. Now she found herself safe from some dangers, but in other ways even worse off, for she was a rebel against the Wizard.

"If so much had not already happened to me, I think I might want to throw myself into the nearest river. That would be a quicker, cleaner death than what the Wolves will give me when they catch me. Yet even the Wolves cannot frighten me that much now. It is also good that you are with me. I do not know what you can do, one man, a traveler who is not even from Rentoro. Yet you have slain three of the Wizard's Wolves. A man who can do that may do many other things."

"Do not hope for too much from me," Blade said. "Certainly I can kill Wolves and I will go on killing them as long as I can. This will certainly do us no harm and the Wizard no good. But it will not keep us alive forever, not with all the Wolves and all the Wizard's friends against us. We must find other answers."

What the answers would be, Blade could still only guess. At least it would be a more intelligent guess than he'd been making before. Lorya had told him a great deal.

She'd implied that the Wizard was one man, but that was

no doubt merely a tale. The terror-filled legends of a century had combined the deeds of three or four men into the single-handed achievement of one immortal superman. So Blade would use "the Wizard" as a sort of mental shorthand, but he'd really mean "the Wizard and his descendants down to the present ruler of Rentoro." He'd been right about the dynasty of tyrants.

Clearly there was something like mental telepathy at work in Rentoro. The "voice that spoke without words" could hardly be anything else. The Wizard controlled workers, commanded the leaders of the Wolves, and perhaps detected rebellion by reading and controlling minds.

Blade did not find it easy to accept the idea or comfortable to live with it. In Home Dimension telepathy was still something for science-fiction stories. A good many experiments had been made, but only the boldest parapsychologists dared claim they'd proved anything positive. Yet here in Rentoro, there was no escaping the evidence. So much fell into place now, even the way the leaders of the Wolves sat on their heudas, looking up at the sky. They were waiting, their minds a blank, to receive their master's telepathic commands!

So much for part of the Wizard's "magic." The other part was a little harder to analyze, at least from what Lorya had told him. Blade was quite willing to believe that the Wolves were comparatively few in number and had won their victories by concentrating with supernatural speed. Nothing else made sense. An army outnumbering the combined forces of all the cities and towns of Rentoro would be impossible for the Wizard. In this medieval economy he could never support it. The Wolves would eat the country bare, until the last man in Rentoro died of starvation and left the Wizard in his castle to rule over a desert that he'd made himself. The Wizard had done many strange and evil things in Rentoro, but he obviously hadn't turned it into a desert.

So a small army of picked troops who moved like the wind was the only answer. How did they move?

The most obvious notion was that the Wizard had some sort of mechanical transport, perhaps airborne. A few large helicopters or transport planes could move a hundred Wolves from one end of Rentoro to the other between dusk and dawn. If no one saw the machines, the swift movement would seem magical.

The notion was obvious, but it had too many holes for

Blade to be happy with it. It would not be easy to conceal the existence of something as large and noisy as a transport plane or a helicopter for a single year, let alone a whole century.

Also, if the Wizard had airplanes, why did he insist on using medieval weapons against the people of Rentoro? He could easily have given the Wolves machine guns, artillery, and rockets. With modern firepower a few hundred Wolves would be enough to rule Rentoro, able to blow apart any city whose people weren't already too scared to lift a finger! They would also be much cheaper than the force of Wolves and heudas the Wizard used now.

So the Wizard did not have airplanes or any other modern method of transport for his army. What did he have? Something, certainly. But what Richard Blade had was an unsolved, and for the time being unsolvable, mystery.

Except—what about those Wolves who'd come to Dodini, apparently *riding out of thin air?* Blade was now reasonably certain that his brain and eyes had both been working properly. So perhaps he'd actually seen what he thought he'd seen—the Wizard's Wolves suddenly emerging from nowhere and charging down the hill toward Dodini.

Unfortunately, that left things nearly as confusing as before. There was such a thing as teleportation—moving oneself through space by pure mental effort. There was also such a thing as telekinesis—moving other objects or people the same way.

Blade mentally corrected himself. These things existed in the *theories* of some parapsychologists.

In Rentoro, did they exist in reality? Did the Wizard have the mental powers to pick up a whole army of mounted and armored men and hurl them hundreds of miles?

That was as hard to accept as the airplanes. If the Wizard had that kind of mental power, he wouldn't need the army. He would be able to stand on a hilltop, say to himself, "Let the walls of Dodini fall down," concentrate his mind—and a thousand miles away the walls of Dodini would crumble into rubble. He didn't do this, although it would be an even more powerful weapon than machine guns or airplanes. Therefore he probably couldn't do it.

But what *did* he do?

Blade shook his head in exasperation. There was no doubt about it. The mystery of the Wizard of Rentoro took the bloody cake, when it came to weird mysteries!

There was also no doubt about what he had to do. He had to seek out the present Wizard himself, whoever the man might be and whatever the dangers involved in approaching him. There was nowhere else to get the answers he needed—although he might not get them even there.

Deciding on his next move was always a load off Blade's mind. He stood up and flexed his arms and legs. Then he asked Lorya, "Do you know the way to the Wizard's castle?" She stared at him, wide-eyed and confused. He laughed. "Never mind. We'll talk about it in the morning. Let's get some sleep."

They curled up under a pile of blankets and spare clothing, snuggling together for warmth. Blade thought he saw a disappointed look on Lorya's face when he only patted her shoulder as he lay down. He ignored it. Neither of them needed anything but a good night's sleep, not after this day and not here in the woods, with the damp earth under them and the wet leaves still shaking down drops on them.

Blade slept and his sleep was filled with strange dreams. He saw himself walking through the streets of London, entering J's office, talking with the man, being called by his full name. Then he saw a burning medieval town and himself standing in front of a pile of blackened timbers that had once been a house. He had the feeling there were many other things, even stranger, but he remembered none of them.

They awoke to find blue sky visible through the branches. The roads would be drying out, speeding their travel and easing the burden on the heuda. It seemed to be in fairly good shape as it browsed quietly on the ferns, but Blade wanted to go on spearing it as much as possible. They had to keep ahead of the Wolves' search and that would be easier mounted than on foot.

The fire was down to ashes. Blade churned the ashes into the damp ground to conceal their campsight while Lorya packed the gear. Then they mounted and rode back on to a trail bathed in sunlight.

As they rode out into the light, Blade threw back his head and opened his mouth. Then he shut it abruptly. There were many things he might have to do in this Dimension, but there was one thing he would *not* do.

He would not sing, whistle, or even hum, "We're Off to See the Wizard."

Chapter 9

Blade planned to stay clear of anything larger than a farming village until both he and Lorya were so heavily disguised that their own mothers wouldn't have recognized them. In the villages and farms there were also men who would bear tales to the Wizard, but not quickly enough to help the Wolves in their search.

To confuse matters further, the Wolves would doubtless expect anyone who'd so openly rebelled against the Wizard to be making a dash for the borders of Rentoro. What lay beyond those borders was unexplored wilderness, with land that would grow no crops and forests swarmed with wild animals and savage cannibals. Here and there a handful of outlaws had carved out a small territory for themselves, but were so busy defending it that the Wizard could afford to ignore them. The borderlands offered nothing to tempt anyone—except a man who'd slain three of the Wolves. He might expect a more merciful death from the outlaws, the bears, or the cannibals than from the Wolves.

Instead, Blade and Lorya would be heading straight for the Wizard's castle, something few sane men in Rentoro ever did. Even those who gladly served the Wizard usually preferred to do so from a safe distance.

But—suppose the Wizard had tapped Blade's mind and read his thoughts? Blade wondered if this could happen without his being aware of it, and thought of last night's dreams. The problem was, he was dealing with a phenomenon far beyond not only his own experience but all of Home Dimension's scientific knowledge. There were no guidelines, only more educated guesswork.

He could be certain that he was nearly impossible to hypnotize. He could suspect that if telepathy existed, it involved something not too far from hypnosis. Therefore a man hard to hypnotize might also be very hard to reach telepathically, at least without his consent. That was as far as he cared to go at the moment. He would assume that neither the Wizard nor the Wolves knew which way he was going—and keep his sword sharp while he rode.

Lorya was uncomfortable with the idea of riding straight on to the Wizard's castle, but not frightened. She trusted Blade's judgment, and in any case a clean death held no real terrors for her. Her objections were all simple, common-sense ones.

"The castle of the Wizard is also the lair of his Wolves. For many miles outside the walls they keep a close watch. How shall we pass through them to reach the castle? Do we slip in by night?"

Blade shook his head. "No. We go in by day. That way no one will think us people who have anything to fear from the Wolves."

"Then the Wolves will surely find us."

"Yes, but we can say that we have business for the Wizard, and for him only."

"Will they believe us?"

"Lorya, I have been in many lands and met several men who behave like the Wizard. Their servants go in mortal fear of displeasing them and would not dare risk turning aside a man who says he has business with their master. Believe me, the Wolves will not lift a finger against us."

"And then? After we enter the castle? What do you hope to do?"

"Meet the Wizard. I am traveling to learn as much as I can about each land I visit."

"Why?"

"I am curious."

Lorya shook her head. "I think a better word might be mad." She laughed. "Perhaps the Wizard will also think you are mad, and let you go."

Blade wasn't sure what he wanted the man to think. Even if the Wizard turned out to have nothing but swordsmen and dungeons at his command, bearding him in his den would be a risky business. If it hadn't been for the strange powers the Wizard might have, Blade would have been quite willing to study him from a safe distance.

Blade and Lorya kept to the trail all morning, then spent the afternoon cutting across country. They camped for the night in the forest a mile from a small village. In the chill darkness of the early morning, Blade slipped into the village and stole a heuda for Lorya. They were on the move again well before daylight, and did not stop until evening, twenty miles away from the village and anybody who might recognize the stolen animal.

That was how they made their way across Rentoro toward the Wizard's castle—one improvisation after another, always with the idea of confusing their trail. Lorya cut her hair short, darkened her skin, and dressed in man's clothing, passing as Blade's servant. Blade acquired one set of clothing after another, each a little fancier than the one before it. He paid for the clothes, for Lorya's saddle, for their food and wine, and for their lodging at inns or farmhouses with pieces of the gold necklace.

Blade did not explain who he was, and no one asked him to do so. Each piece of the necklace was worth a year's wages for a skilled worker. No sensible man would risk losing that much money by asking pointless questions.

There was another reason for people's lack of curiosity, as Lorya explained. "In Rentoro, a man like you, who travels without saying why, is almost always high in the service of the Wizard. Such men often take lodging, meals, heudas, even women as their natural right. If one of them is generous enough to pay, no Rentoran in his senses is going to argue."

Rentorans might not go to the Wizard's castle, but even the children knew where it was. Day after day the directions grew more precise, and day after day Blade pushed on faster. An eagerness to get to grips with the Wizard and dig out his secrets was beginning to fill him. Lorya saw this and found it more and more difficult to hide her doubts. Sometimes Blade caught a glimpse of her when she didn't think he was looking, and her face was drawn and troubled. Dark circles grew under her eyes, and flesh melted off her already slim body.

On the eleventh day they reached the last village on the road to the castle. South of the village, white wooden posts with the wolf sign in green rose on either side of the road. They marked the beginning of the area patrolled by the Wolves. No man willingly passed those posts without some very good reason, and not all those who did came out again.

The village itself was no more than a dozen houses, four of them inns with stables attached. The inns all looked prosperous, for there was money to be earned from the Wizard's servants as they passed back and forth on their master's business. But even that money could not make men happy about living here in the Wizard's back yard, with the Wolves never more than half an hour's ride away. All the men and women in the village had a hunted look, and there were only a few children.

Blade stopped in sight of the village, but well out of earshot of any of its people, and motioned Lorya up close beside him.

"We spend the night here," he said. "Then I ride on, to the Wizard's castle."

"Alone?" Her eyes widened. "But I—"

"Let me finish. I hope to be back within ten days, for better or worse. If I am not back within ten days—"

"I can ride in after you."

"No. Wait another five days. Something quite harmless may have happened to delay me. At the end of the extra five days, sell everything you can spare and ride north as fast as you can. Find some town where no one knows you and use the rest of the gold to settle there. Perhaps you may be able to return to Dodini someday, but it will not be safe for a year or two at least.

"If I'm not back in fifteen days, one of two things will have happened. Either I'll be dead, or I'll have had to flee so quickly that I'd be putting you in danger by trying to pick you up. Either way, you won't do anything by going to the castle except fall into the hands of the Wolves and throw your life away for nothing."

The woman seemed about to protest, but Blade raised a hand and continued. "Lorya, you've had more than your share of bad luck in your life. But that life isn't over and your luck could change. Give it a chance, why don't you, instead of getting yourself killed at twenty?"

Lorya said nothing, but her hands were shaking slightly and she kept her head carefully turned away from Blade. He did not feel particularly good about having to leave Lorya behind, to wait in an agony of suspense while he faced the Wizard, but there was nothing to justify taking her any farther into danger.

He could see now that he'd made a mistake in taking Lorya with him this far. Yet it would have been death to leave her in Dodini, and he hadn't realized she might come to care for him the way she obviously had. Damn! He'd been remarkably slow in a matter where he was usually alert. Now he'd contrived to drag another innocent person deep into danger, after swearing a mighty oath he'd do everything he could to avoid this happening again!

He urged his heuda forward. "Come on, Lorya. Let's see what the inns have in the way of wine. They've got to have something better than the purple vinegar we drank last night!"

Blade came up the winding stairs, hearing the wood creak under his weight and ducking his head to get under the low beams. The stairs were swept clean of dust, but still smelled of old wine, unwashed human bodies, and the oil from the dim, guttering lamps that shed a faint orange light.

Blade reached the top of the stairs and turned right, down the hall leading to the inn's half-dozen private rooms. To the left were the three large communal chambers, each with beds for a dozen people. Blade thought of sticking his head inside one, to see what kind of people were snoring away there, then decided against it. In this village people were very careful to keep to themselves, not asking others' business or even meeting others' eyes.

Blade decided he would not ask Lorya to wait for him here. A few hours in the grim atmosphere of this village was already making him edgy. Two weeks of it would make the poor woman a nervous wreck. He'd send her ten miles back up the road to the village of Peloff and the Inn of the Blue Swan. She could wait more safely and much more comfortably there.

Blade reached his room, turned the huge iron key in the lock, pushed the door open, then stopped abruptly. The sleeping pallet beside the bed where Lorya had been lying was empty. He scanned the room quickly. The candle still burned in the candlestick by the head of the bed, and everything else was as it had been when he left. But the room was as completely empty as if Lorya had been spirited away by magic.

Blade's hand went to the hilt of his sword and he took a step forward, surprise and the beginnings of fear rising in him. The fear was not for himself, but for Lorya. Had the Wizard's powers reached out and struck at her, or had human agents come after her? He drew his dagger and took another step forward, trying to look in all directions at once. Possibly—

Then Blade heard the unmistakable sound of a deep breath

from behind the door, the only part of the room his eyes couldn't reach. He froze in mid-stride, then started to turn. A moment later came an unmistakable, uncontrollable giggle. Blade whirled around and slammed the door behind him. Lorya stood there, shaking with laughter that she was vainly trying to keep silent. She was shaking so hard that she had to brace herself against the wall to keep from collapsing on the floor.

She was also entirely nude.

Blade's breath went out of him in a whistle of pleased surprise. Then he wanted to laugh at himself. A fine spectacle he must have been, entering the room as though a hungry tigher waited to leap out at him. No wonder Lorya finally broke into giggles! Of course it was a dangerous joke to play on a man with his training, who became a deadly fighting machine the moment his suspicions were aroused. But he didn't have to tell her this and spoil her fun, not on this evening, the last time they might ever see each other.

So he said nothing. Instead he stepped forward, bent, and swept her up into his arms. She let her head drop back, arching her neck and exposing her throat to Blade's lips. He noticed that her breath was coming fast, and a tendon in the slim neck was vibrating like a plucked harpstring.

This didn't surprise Blade at all. When he raised his lips from her throat, his own breath was coming in gasps, as if he'd just run a couple of miles at top speed. His strength seemed to have doubled so that he was holding Lorya, not a small woman in spite of her slenderness, as easily as if she'd been a child.

He held her for a moment longer, then turned, carried her over to the bed, and laid her down on the quilt. She lay on her back, her arms at her side and her breasts rising and falling with her quick breathing. She kept her eyes fixed on Blade as he pulled off his clothes. In the dim light those eyes seemed to be twice their normal size and Blade could have sworn they were glowing like a cat's.

Lorya suddenly wriggled and laughed softly. "I wonder what anyone would say if he could spy on us—the Wizard's man and his 'servant.' Of course, some of the Wizard's men are said to have a liking for boys."

"They might wonder at first," Blade said, smiling. "But not for long. No one who got a good look at you could think for a moment you're a boy."

That was nothing less than the truth. Lorya was fine-boned and slender, almost lean. She'd had little spare flesh to begin with and the long journey across Rentoro had taken off much of that. Yet she was still beautiful, her breasts shallow but exquisite cones with dark nipples now risen into points, her belly extraordinarily taut and flat for a woman who'd borne a child, her legs simply breathtaking—long for her height, strongly muscled, exquisitely molded. Those legs drew Blade's attention until he had to sit down on the bed beside Lorya and run his hands up and down them, from the feet up to the inner thighs and back down again. Under his hands her skin was firm, and seemed to be cool and warm at the same time.

Gradually his hands spent more time on her inner thighs, occasionally brushing lightly over the triangle of fine dark hair nestling between them. As Blade's hands worked, so did his lips, kissing Lorya's eyes, ears, and lips, again caressing her throat, working down to her breasts and across the skin of her belly until she shivered and moaned.

Lorya did not lie quietly under Blade's hands and lips. Far from it. Her own hands were making their own thorough exploration of his body, and her lips pressed against his as if she wanted to weld the two of them together. In the brief moments when her arms went around him, he could feel her wiry strength, feel her trembling, feel her nails digging into his skin.

At last there was no part of each other's bodies they hadn't explored with lips and hands. Lorya was quivering from head to foot, her eyes were closed, and from her open mouth came a steady whimpering. Blade's own breath rasped in his throat like sand, and his groin seemed to be glowing white hot. His lips returned to Lorya's throat again. She caught him with both arms, hands gripping his hair. He wanted to slip gently into her, but instead her legs seemed to fly apart and her hands tightened, dragging him down, dragging him deep within her in a single fierce moment.

Now her legs rose and locked around Blade's waist, while her hands slipped down onto his back. Her nails dug in deeper than before, but Blade felt no pain. He couldn't have felt pain if he and Lorya had been hurled into a boiling cauldron. He could feel nothing but Lorya, swamping all his senses, enveloping him, surrounding his mind as she'd already surrounded part of his body.

He was slow to feel anything else. He was dimly aware

that Lorya was moving under him as he moved within her, that her legs were clamping tighter and her hands were once again in his hair. He heard her moans rise and he heard his own breath coming faster and faster. Yet he was less aware than usual of the slow equisite climb toward the final release, the quickening, the twisting, his desperate efforts to hold back and the woman's desperate efforts to push on to the end.

He still knew when the release came. It came so nearly at the same moment for both of them that Blade and Lorya couldn't have said who was first, even if they'd cared about knowing.

They only cared that Lorya had to bite back a scream, then went completely rigid, arms and legs frozen. Blade gave a thick, gasping cry, and his powerful body thrashed and jerked. He cried out again, Lorya's breath hissed out of her body in one long sigh, then her teeth met in his ear as his head sank down on her breast.

They were a long time in that position, neither of them entirely conscious. Somehow Blade's weight did not crush Lorya underneath him and somehow she did not cry out from his pressing upon her. Finally they untangled themselves, but had neither the strength nor the desire to move far apart. Blade managed to pull the quilt over them before sleep took him.

They awoke at the dreariest hour of dawn and Blade found that Lorya's desire was also awakened. His brief thoughts of pushing her away lasted only until her hands and lips went to work. Then they came together with a passion as great as the night's, and far more tender. This time Lorya wept as she lay in Blade's arms afterward. Blade himself would not have greatly minded hearing that the Wizard of Rentoro was dead and his castle fallen into rubble.

By the time they came downstairs, it was several hours into a gray, windy morning. Everyone else at the inn had already eaten breakfast, and the innkeeper grumbled about "slug-a-beds" as he served them porridge, cheese, and wine.

Then there was nothing to do but go outside, pack their gear, and ride off on their separate ways. They were back in their disguises as an agent of the Wizard and his servant, so there could be no affectionate farewells. Lorya mounted her heuda and rode off toward the north without a backward look. Blade watched until the slender, stiff-backed figure was out of sight in the misty rain that was starting to fall. Then he turned and looked the other way, down the road to where the white posts marked the beginning of the Wizard's personal territory. He mounted and spurred his heuda into movement.

He'd done his best for Lorya. She was on her way to the safest place within easy reach. She had the skill and determination she'd need to survive whatever happened to him, and she had all the rest of the gold.

He'd thought of taking some himself, but why bother? If the Wizard and the Wolves gave him a friendly reception, he wouldn't need money. If they didn't—well, he'd either be on his way out of the Wizard's lands so fast he wouldn't be stopping to pay for anything, or he would never be going anywhere or paying for anything again.

Chapter 10

Blade rode past the white posts at a canter, then slowed to a trot as soon as they were out of sight behind him. He wanted to spare the heuda even more than usual. He might have to ride for his life before this day was over, and he wanted his mount as fresh as possible.

It was two hours before Blade saw a single Wolf. During those two hours he rode steadily onward, stopping twice to let the heuda catch its breath. He rode with his sword belted on over his coat, ready at hand, and with one dagger in his boot and another up one sleeve. His crossbow was slung on one side of his saddle and a bag of bolts for it on the other side. He wasn't sure if the Wizard's agents ever rode up armed to the teeth like this, but he didn't care. In Blade's experience, few men ever died from having too many weapons ready to use.

The road was wide enough for three men to ride abreast and surfaced with hard-packed gravel. It twisted and turned in curves and sharp bends. Some of these curves and bends took it around hills or ravines. Others seemed intended to bring it within easy range of perfect ambush sites.

Twice Blade crossed small wooden bridges. He noticed that the roadbed of each bridge was made of loose planks, while the supports were held together by ropes and wedges. A dozen trained men could take this bridge apart in an hour, using nothing but their bare hands. An invader could still push cavalry and infantry across the stream and on across country. He could not do the same with the heavy wagons carrying food or siege equipment.

Just beyond the second bridge, Blade came to a farm, perched on a hill beside a bend in the road. Its fields were masses of rank weeds and its barn was a sagging pile of decaying timber. No one had raised a crop here for many

56

years. Yet the farm still had its uses as part of the Wizard's defense plans.

The walls of the farmhouse were loopholed for crossbows. A stout brick wall surrounded the farmyard. Near the top, black iron spikes, sharp and freshly painted, jutted outward from the brick. A wooden barrier crowned the wall and it also was loopholed. In the center of the farmyard rose a circular stone tower with a tiled wooden cupola and a weathervane on top.

Over the past century the Wizards of Rentoro had created a formidable defense in depth. Spies and Wolves made rebellion almost impossible, but the Wizards still weren't taking any chances.

By luck or through the Wizard's mistakes a rebel army might assemble and march on the castle. It would not be able to use the Wizard's roads. Instead it would be forced to disperse and scatter across the country as it marched. Then the Wolves, concentrating with their unnatural speed, would come down on the scattered columns. An invader would be lucky to get within sight of the castle's walls.

At least Blade could now understand why he hadn't met any Wolves on the road. With these defenses stretching for miles ahead of him, there was no need to hurry in stopping a lone rider. The Wolves would be waiting for him where they could do so most comfortably, and they would speak to him when they found it convenient.

The farm disappeared around the bend of the road. Blade trotted into a forest and the heuda began to labor slightly as the road climbed a hill. Half a mile farther on he came out of the forest, back into the gray daylight, and found the Wolves waiting for him.

There were only three of them—one of the leaders and two men-at-arms. The men-at-arms wore their usual armor and weapons, but the leader was dressed more for dancing than for fighting. He wore a black tunic embroidered with gold and with silver lacing down the front, blue hose, a flowing red cloak with a fur collar—in general, the clothes of a Renaissance nobleman on his way to a party. A white sash around the man's thick waist supported a blue-enameled wolf's-head badge and a jeweled dagger.

The face above the lace collar was less elegant. It was tanned, scarred, coarsened by years of too much food and wine, but still hard and ugly. It was a face Blade had seen

57

many times—the professional mercenary, without scruples, friends, or any place in the world except what he can win by his sword and loyalty to his chief. A dangerous man in a fight, but otherwise more accustomed to obeying orders than to making up his own mind, and therfore perhaps less dangerous to Blade here and now.

Blade rode straight up to the three Wolves, paying no more attention to them than to the rain. He pulled to a stop twenty feet away, just as the leader started toward him. One of the men-at-arms drew his sword, while the other unslung his crossbow.

"The Wizard gives you welcome," said the leader. His voice matched his face—rough, harsh, and much less polite than his choice of words.

"I come on the affairs of the Wizard," said Blade. Only a Wolf or an agent who'd served the Wizard for many years would use the forbidden proper name without betraying himself by nervousness or hesitation.

The man nodded. "It is written?" he went on, pointing at Blade's saddlebags.

"It is here," said Blade, pointing at his forehead. "It is for the Wizard, and none other."

"That may be," said the man. "It comes from—where?"

"From Morina," said Blade. "Some also from near Dodini." He'd picked those two cities well in advance. Dodini must have been giving the Wizard trouble, or the Wolves would not have attacked it. Thanks to Lorya he also knew a good deal about the place.

He knew little about Morina, but he knew one important thing—it was still the most closely watched city in Rentoro. The present Wizard had not forgotten its leadership of the last rebellion against the first Wizard's authority. Nor had Morina forgotten the slaughter of its people by the Wolves when the rebellion was put down. News from Morina should be something no Wolf would care to delay a single moment.

The Wolf nodded and was silent for a moment, his eyes still on Blade. Blade returned the Wolf's stare, and did his best to hide the tension he felt. He was on a hair trigger, alert for the slightest sign of the leader's receiving a command from the Wizard or of the two men-at-arms going into action.

The silence lasted until Blade was almost certain that something had gone wrong and he was going to be hurled into a vicious little fight. He was fairly sure he could deal with these three, but after that—

The Wolf leader turned toward his men and waved one hand. They spurred their heudas up to Blade, and one of them took out of a pouch on his belt a two-foot length of red ribbon. On it were embroidered three golden wolves, one running, one standing, and only lying, as well as several words in a script Blade didn't recognize. The leader tied the ribbon to the bridle of Blade's heuda, then raised a hand in farewell. "Pass on to the Wizard," he said.

Blade had to fight an impulse to spur his heuda to a full gallop and hold that pace until he was out of bowshot. Instead he kept the heuda to a leisurely trot until the Wolves were out of sight around a bend in the road.

So far so good. The Wolf leader had passed him on as someone with legitimate business here, or at least not dangerous enough to stop. He'd also been given what he hoped was a safe-conduct pass, but which might be a "shoot this man on sight" message to the next band of Wolves.

Apparently the ribbon was a safe-conduct. The next three bands of Wolves Blade met stopped him, looked at the ribbon, then waved him on. Each time he kept expecting a crossbow bolt to sprout in his back, until he was out of sight or at least out of easy range.

The country was growing more rugged, with rocky hills, a few stunted trees, and cliffs overhanging the road at nearly every curve. Along this stretch, a hundred Wolves could hold off an army of ten thousand simply by rolling rocks down from the cliffs. Then suddenly the road made a hairpin turn around a last cliff. On the other side a solid stone bridge ran across a deep ravine. Beyond the ravine lush fields of grain rolled away toward a long black wall. Far away beyond the wall Blade saw four round towers. One gleamed faintly as a stray sunbeam broke through the clouds and struck the polished tiles on the domed roof.

Blade spurred his heuda to a gallop. His cloak streamed out behind him as he thundered across the bridge and down the winding road, past fields of grain swaying in the wind. There were people at work in the fields—old men and even older women, or so it seemed to Blade as he swept by. Then at last the black wall loomed before him, rising fifty feet above the stone-paved square in front of the gate.

He had reached the castle of the Wizard of Rentoro.

Seen close up, the castle was even larger than Blade had imagined it from Lorya's tales. What he could see of it showed signs of neglect. Vines grew all the way to the top of the wall, and there was a foot-wide crack thirty feet high to the right of the gate. Grass sprouted from the cracks in the stone under him.

The Wizard might be getting careless, but Blade doubted it. Even if an enemy did manage to reach the castle's walls, it would take them so long the Wizard would have plenty of time to put his house in order. Meanwhile, what was the sense in spending money and labor on things that might never be needed? The Wizard could not create workers out of thin air, or feed and clothe them with a wave of his hand.

Blade scanned the wall as far as his eyes could reach, looking for the sentries who must be up there on top of the wall. He couldn't see anyone, but he refused to believe the wall was completely deserted. Sooner or later, someone would come down to open the gate for him.

Time passed, minute after slow minute. The rain slackened and finally stopped, and the wind died to a faint breeze. The storm was also passing.

Now Blade had been waiting outside the castle for close to an hour. The clouds overhead were beginning to break up, but the sunlight revealed no sign of life on the wall. The gate still loomed above him, twenty feet high and thirty feet wide, made of whole tree trunks bound with iron, hung on iron hinges. The wood smelled of grease and the ironwork shone with oil and fresh paint. No neglect here!

In the middle of the left-hand gate was a small postern, a door just high and wide enough for a man about Blade's size to pass through without stooping. On an impulse Blade went over to the postern gate and pulled on the iron ring hanging in the center of it.

With a faint squeal and groan, the postern swung open.

Blade could harldy have been more surprised if the Wizard himself had suddenly materialized in a puff of smoke and a clap of thunder. He also felt rather foolish. He wondered if anyone had been standing up on top of the wall, laughing himself silly at the spectacle of Richard Blade waiting for someone to let him through an unlocked gate.

A less pleasant question popped into his mind as well. Could the Wizard be expecting him?

Blade dismounted, led his heuda over to the nearest vine, and tethered it to a tough brown stalk. Then he drew his sword, walked back to the postern, and stepped through it into the Wizard's castle.

Chapter 11

Blade found himself in a shadowy, musty gateway, so long that it was almost a tunnel. In the dim light it was easy to imagine the heavy stones of the arched roof overhead crashing down on him. Blade hurried toward the open postern visible in the inner gate.

He was three steps from the postern when two things happened. First, the postern slammed shut, sending echoes rolling ominously from the stone walls on either side. Blade had just time to take a deep breath, then there was a rumble from overhead, a *wsssh* of air, and a huge block of stone plunged out of nowhere and smashed into the pavement. In the confined space the impact sounded like an explosion. The echoes doubled and redoubled, while chunks of stone flew in all directions like fragments from an exploding shell. One grazed Blade's leg hard enough to draw blood, while another knocked his sword out of his hand. He picked it up and looked at the stone. If he'd been six feet to the left, he would have been squashed under it like a stepped-on cockroach.

He drew his boot knife and probed the closed postern. There was no ring, latch, or lock visible on the inside. It appeared to be securely fastened from the outside, as if by—

No. Blade made up his mind. He would not let himself start thinking in terms of magic, even if this was a Wizard's castle. There would be a natural explanation for everything that might happen to him.

Blade backed away from the postern, eyes and ears probing the darkness around him. The postern in the outer gate was still open, but he certainly wasn't going to retreat at the first trick the Wizard played on him. Blade darted to the fallen stone and snatched up the largest piece he could lift with one hand. Then he went back to the outer gate, keeping close to the wall. He reached the outer postern and wedged the stone firmly under the open door. That would force anybody who wanted to close it to do the job by hand, rather than by some concealed mechanism. Blade straightened up and turned back toward the inner gate. As he did so, the locked inner postern suddenly swung open.

Blade retraced his steps, knife drawn and hand on sword hilt. If the door started closing this time, he was going to ram his sword into the gap, then go to work on the hinges with the knife.

The postern stayed open, and Blade slipped through. He took a deep breath, then another—then threw himself flat on the ground and rolled furiously to the right. *Sssst-whuk!* Something flashed overhead and struck the gate behind him. Blade twisted around without raising his head and looked.

Four heavy arrows stood quivering in the gate. Each had a wooden shaft a yard long and a solid iron head almost sunk out of sight in the logs. If any of them had hit him, he would have been pinned against the gate, dead without a twitch or a cry.

Behind Blade towered the inner face of the main wall. On two sides rose vine-overgrown brick walls, on the third a line of squat trees with a timber palisade visible beyond them. The palisade was open at one end. There was no one in sight.

The inner postern was still open, but once again Blade was determined not to retreat. Instead he rose, first to hands and knees, then to a sitting position, then to a crouch. When this drew no reaction, he sprang to his feet and dashed across the open ground toward the gap in the palisade.

He dashed through the gap and saw a wide muddy ditch open before him. He was tempted to simply plough a way down one side and up the other, but instinct told him firmly that he shouldn't. So he leaped, soaring across the ditch and landing in waist-high grass on the other side. The grass not only broke his fall, it concealed him almost completely. He lay there to catch his breath.

As he did, part of the muddy bottom of the ditch seemed to come alive. The snake was a good ten feet long and a foot thick, with a triangular head and a body that showed mottled gray and purple under the mud. Blade was quite certain that if he'd walked across the ditch instead of leaping, he would have learned the hard way that the snake was as poisonous as it looked.

He rose and moved on. Someone was almost certainly watching him. He wished he knew why. He did know that he wasn't going to show fear, frustration, or carelessness if he could possibly avoid it.

Somehow, for some incomprehensible purpose of the Wizard of Rentoro, he was being tested. He was going to pass the test or die trying. In fact, that was probably all he could do, other than turn his back on the castle and the Wizard and admit defeat.

All that afternoon Blade pitted himself against the Wizard's tests and traps. He began to feel that he was in a world apart, a world where ordinary concepts of time and space had no meaning. The only constants were the sense of being watched and the certainty that danger lay close at hand.

He might have lost all track of time if the Wizard's testing ground hadn't been open to the sky. The clearing of the sky and then the slow fading of the sunlight told him of the passing hours.

There were tests of agility, there were tests of speed, there were tests of sheer brute strength—lifting a two-hundred pound beam that barred his only way forward. Each of these tests of his physical qualities also tested his ability to think quickly and logically, keep his head, and *keep going forward*. The Wizard's deadly maze was always offering him a safe road back, and he was always refusing to take it.

There was no sign of human activity—in fact, no sign that the huge castle hadn't been swept clean of all human life by a plague. Yet Blade's instincts told him that each test took place under the eye of some hidden observer, ready to tell the Wizard if Blade succeeded, or come out to pick up the mangled remains if he failed. By the time Blade reached the castle, the Wizard would know as much about his skill and strength as anyone could want to know.

The Wizard must have been expecting him. It was hard to believe that he ran every agent coming to bring a report through this deadly obstacle course. That would kill off half his loyal people in a few months. No doubt the agents were met outside the castle and guided in, or had an easier route. Blade, on the other hand, was coming—or being sent—through the jaws of one trap after another. This could hardly be an accident.

It began to be clear that his course was taking him in a spiral, approaching the inner citadel by gradual stages. If he'd been moving in a straight line, he would have reached the citadel long ago. He began to wonder how much farther he had to go.

He also began to wonder how much longer it would be safe to move. The day was fading into twilight and Blade did not wish to face the rest of the obstacle course in the darkness. The night would hide too many subtle warnings of the traps.

He liked even less the idea of just sitting down and waiting for dawn. He hadn't seen any more of the big snakes, but he was sure they or equally unpleasant creatures were close at hand. If he sat down to wait out the darkness, would the Wizard send them out to pay him a visit? He'd have to be awake and on the alert every minute of the night, even if he wasn't on the move.

Blade decided he'd better scramble up on top of one of the walls and get his bearings, rather than plod on through the maze like a white rat in a laboratory. This might be cheating, and it might draw the attention of the Wizard or the Wolves. It still seemed a better idea than simply waiting for night to fall.

Around the next bend lay a paved triangular courtyard, with no signs of traps or obstacles. Close to one wall grew a gnarled, heavy-branched tree. Blade hurried toward it. The tree might have been made to order as a route up the wall.

In the fading light, even Blade's keen eyes could not see that the crack around one section of four paving stones was wider than usual. His foot came down squarely on the one farthest to the left. With a squeal and a crash, all four stones vanished under Blade, as an iron plate supporting them swung down on its hinges. Suddenly there was nothing but empty air and a black shaft under Richard Blade, and he plunged out of sight.

His drawn sword crashed against the edge of the shaft and the shock broke his grip on it. Before he had time to regret the loss, he landed with a thud on some thickly carpeted surface.

The fall rammed the crossbow into Blade's back, knocking all the wind out of him. He lay, unable to move for a moment, while around him in the darkness iron and wood squealed and creaked and groaned like a chorus of madmen.

Suddenly the surface under Blade shuddered violently, then tilted. He fell, this time landing on his side. He wriggled around until he could reach the crossbow and unsling it. As

65

he pulled back the cocking lever, more squealing and groaning sounded overhead.

As Blade watched, a trapdoor swung down, leaving a gaping hole fifteen feet on a side. High above, Blade could see the evening sky, the branches of a tree, and a tower of the Wizard's citadel. Then something else went *click*, the surface under him vibrated—and with a terrific *whang* it snapped upward.

Blade soared up out of the hole in the ground like a rocket. At the top of his climb he found he'd parted company with his crossbow. Twisting in midair, he saw he was flying toward a row of thorny-looking bushes, with a broad expanse of something black and shiny beyond them. He twisted again, desperately trying to bring himself down into the bushes. They'd probably tear off half his skin, but the alternative was landing beyond them on the black surface. It looked like polished stone, and hitting it from this height would break half his bones.

Blade plunged down, knew a sickening moment of realizing he was going to hit the black surface, then struck it. It wasn't stone, but inky water, deep and icy cold. He plunged far under, then came to the surface sputtering and gasping.

As he sucked in a deep breath, he realized there was a strong current in the water, carrying him across the pond. He tried to swim, realized the current was too strong, and found himself being swept over the lip of a small dam. It sloped steeply down and vanished in shadow far below. He could not see the bottom, but he could see a wooden footbridge running across the face of the dam. From under the footbridge iron spikes jutted downward, the water foaming about their points. Anyone coming down the face of the dam would be impaled on the spikes, unless they flattened themselves enough to pass under.

Blade had only a few seconds to realize his situation, then a few more to act as the water swept him along. He squeezed himself as flat as possible, until his head was under the water. Pain seared across the top of his head as one spike gouged his scalp. Then he was past the barrier, sliding down into the shadows. He raised his head, took a deep breath, and in the next moment plunged out into thin air again.

This was the longest fall of all and Blade had time to wonder if it was going to be the last one of his life. Then he plunged into another icy pool with a splash so loud that it was still echoing from the stone walls as his head broke the surface.

Before Blade could do anything more, a metallic clank sounded from high overhead, then suddenly light flared close at hand. The glare after so much darkness half-dazzled Blade. It was a moment before he could make out a ledge at the side of the pool, glistening gray walls rising all around him, and seven fully armed Wolves standing on the ledge.

Blade saw at once there was no way out of there except past the Wolves and through a doorway at the rear of the ledge. He swam to the ledge and heaved himself out of the water. He stood up, water dripping from him, keeping his hands carefully in view and well away from his knife. He took a step forward, the Wolf leader waved his arms, and the six men-at-arms ran at Blade.

Blade had no time to see that the Wolves were coming at him barehanded. All he could see was that, after all he'd gone through, the Wolves were going to slaughter him. He'd never see the Wizard of Rentoro. It had all been wasted.

So rage filled him and he let out a roar of sheer fury that made even the Wolf leader jump. As the echoes of that roar boomed around the cave, Blade leaped forward, his knife rasping out and gleaming in the torchlight. He slashed at one Wolf, wheeling as he did to aim a kick at the groin of a second.

The knife sprayed sparks as it grated across the man's helmet, then drew a spurt of blood as it opened his cheek. Blade's kick missed the second man's groin, but slammed into his thigh hard enough to knock him off balance. He staggered into the path of a third Wolf, both men went down together, and Blade leaped on them.

He drove a booted foot down on a man's throat, felt bone and cartilage shatter, heard the man scream. He whirled as two men tried to grab his arms, his clubbed hands smashing both of them aside. He kicked one man in the knee and chopped him in the back of the neck as he screamed and tried to hop away on one leg. He fought like a mad robot, hammering and kicking and stabbing, until the floor ran with the blood of the Wolves and his own fists and arms were raw and bloody from pounding on steel armor.

He fought, until a Wolf got behind him for just long

enough. Then pain and fire exploded in his head, he was briefly aware of staggering and falling, knew that he was lying on the floor helpless—and finally stopped knowing anything at all.

Chapter 12

Blade awoke in a canopied bed large enough for six people, under a pile of quilts thick enough to keep him warm at the North Pole. Every muscle in his body was complaining and he was bruised and scraped all over, as if he'd taken a quick trip through a cement mixer.

None of this was enough to keep him in bed. Blade rolled out of bed and did a few exercises. If it came to a fight, he would do well enough. Anything less than a strong force of Wolves in top shape was going to get badly mauled if they tried anything.

With an effort, he forced himself out of this bloodthirsty mood. Why assume he was going to have to fight again, when he didn't know what orders the Wizard had given? He now realized that the Wolves had taken him prisoner, when they could have easily chopped him to pieces and fed him to the castle's watchdogs. They'd taken him with their bare hands, and some of them had been killed doing this. He'd been allowed to reach the end of his long journey alive, well, and fit to meet the Wizard. Quite probably the Wizard of Rentoro didn't want him killed.

His mind settled on this point, Blade began to inspect his room. It was one of those rooms that made him wonder if he was a guest or a prisoner. The walls were hung with tapestries, the floor covered with fleeces and furs, the bed and the other furniture richly carved out of some pale hardwood. In one corner was a silver watertap and a wooden stand with two jeweled cups, in another corner a marble toilet.

There were also bars on the one high narrow window, iron rings hanging from the walls, and a door of solid iron, heavy enough to stop a tank. He was going to be quite comfortable in this room—but he was also going to be staying in it, whether he liked it or not, until someone outside let him leave.

After three days without food or clothing, Blade began to wonder just how comfortable he was supposed to be. He'd heard and seen nothing to suggest the castle was even inhabited. He knew it was, but he now knew as well that the Wizard and his men were ignoring his existence.

Maybe they hoped to weaken him by hunger, but they wouldn't find that easy. It would be another week before they could hope to find him seriously weakened. Until then, he would be both willing and able to put up a fight. His original bloodthirsty mood was beginning to return, stronger than before.

After another three days without food, Blade's stomach shrank down and its angry rumblings stopped. Blade's mood was more savage than ever. He was about ready to kill the first person who stepped through the door, then tear him apart, roast him over a fire of tapestries and furniture, and eat him!

Blade laughed at the vision this thought conjured up. In a few more days, his situation would no longer be a laughing matter. He would start losing strength, until he would be an easy victim for even one Wolf, let alone half a dozen. Eventually he would start losing his willpower and self-control. Then what? He might not actually go mad, but he could become horribly vulnerable to whatever the Wizard might do to him. He was more vulnerable to hypnosis when his system was depressed by drugs, fatigue, illness, or hunger. Would he also be more vulnerable to the Wizard's mental powers? Would the Wizard be able to strip his mind of all defenses, extract its contents like the meat from a coconut, and turn him into a helpless puppet? Would the Wizard—

Whatever the Wizard might do, he, Richard Blade, would spend no more time worrying about it. The six days of hunger must already be working on him, if he could let his mind spin horrifying fantasies this way.

The Wizards of Rentoro might once have been telepaths. In fact, Blade was prepared to believe they had been. But what about the present Wizard? Everything about the way he wielded his power over Rentoro could be explained without telepathy. Even the trances of the Wolf leaders could be nothing more than a ritual of meditation. With enough men loyal to him, the Wizard could give the appearance of having all the "magical" powers of his ancestors.

Still, telepathy or not, if the Wizard did not come within

the next week, he would find Blade helpless, physcially and perhaps mentally. What would happen then, Blade didn't care to guess, and firmly put any further wild fantasies out of his mind.

That night Blade enjoyed his best sleep since reaching the castle. He woke with a memory of strange dreams, to hear an almost equally strange sound. It was an iron key, turning in the lock of the door.

Blade sprang out of bed as the door opened. He crouched behind the bed as five Wolf leaders in full armor clanked into the room. Then he rose to face the man who followed the Wolves into the room.

His journey was *really* over. At last he was in the presence of the Wizard of Rentoro.

The man had to be the Wizard of Rentoro. It was hard to imagine anyone else being escorted about the castle by five Wolf leaders. Nonetheless, the man's appearance was something of a surprise.

Blade hadn't expected a Hollywood version of Merlin the Magician—long robe, high pointed cap, long flowing white beard, staff with mysterious carvings on it. Neither had he expected anything like the man who stood before him, arms crossed on his chest and dark face set in a tight, formal smile.

The Wizard seemed to be about Blade's own age—no longer young, but still in the prime of life. He stood just under six feet, barrel-chested, heavy-boned, with large powerful hands and legs like tree trunks. Large dark eyes stared at Blade over a hooked nose. The massive chin appeared even heavier due to a square-cut black beard, oiled and faintly perfumed. The Wizard wore a black velvet tunic with slashed and puffed sleeves, skin-tight hose with one leg green and the other white, red leather shoes with long points, and a sash of gilded metal links. A long dagger with a silver hilt in the shape of a wolf's head was thrust into the sash.

The man had an air about him that Blade found hard to define. There was no single word to describe it, there was only a list of the qualities that seemed to be in the man. Ruthlessness, alertness, determination, and sheer strength were all part of him. Blade suspected that right now the Wizard could be more than his match in unarmed combat. The more he looked at the Wizard, the more the man made him think of some great nobleman of the Italian Renaissance—perhaps a

71

mercenary captain who'd fought his way up to rule a city, a man who could admire an exquisite statue one day and order a dozen men out for execution the next. Even without any telepathic powers, this man would not be easy to either fight or deceive.

Then the Wizard spoke. He spoke in the Rentoran language, with an accent that reminded Blade of something from Home Dimension. He was trying to remember what it reminded him of when he heard the Wizard's last words:

"—so I am pleased to bid you welcome, Richard Blade."

The shock of hearing his name from the Wizard jerked Blade's attention back to the man standing in front of him. It was just in time. A moment later Blade sensed a message passing into his mind, filling it like an echoing shout in a cave.

"Open your thoughts to me," was the message. "Open them, and let me know them. I am not your enemy."

Fortunately Blade had been warned that he might be facing telepathy and other paranormal powers. So he was not caught unprepared or ignorant of what was happening, and that saved his mind if not his life.

The Wizard gave Blade no more than a few seconds to consider the request and reply to it. Then he struck with all the power of his mind, and Blade felt in that blow the anger of a proud man who takes the slightest resistance as not only a crime but a personal insult. The Wizard was as jealous of his supremacy over the inner world of the mind as he was of his supremacy over the outer world of Rentoro.

Blade knew that he had to resist. The Wizard was hardly likely to stop with merely reading Blade's thoughts. He would go on to plant his own, until there was nothing in Blade's mind the Wizard hadn't put there—or at least nothing to keep the Wizard from controlling all of Blade's actions.

Blade knew he had to keep his mind totally occupied with his own thoughts, so there would be no room for the Wizard to plant any of his deadly messages. He would also have to fight this battle entirely on the defensive. He hoped he could keep the Wizard's thoughts out of his mind, but he had no chance of pushing any of his own thoughts into the Wizard's mind.

All this ran through Blade's thoughts in seconds. Then he settled down to his mental duel with the Wizard.

His first thought was a defiant shout against the Wizard's call, "I am not your enemy."

You are a liar! Blade mentally shouted.

You are a liar!

You are a liar!

Blade hurled that thought through his mind over and over again, more and more intensely as he felt the Wizard trying to interrupt him. If he'd been saying the words, he would have been shouting them at the top of his lungs.

You are a liar.

You must not fight me. I am not your enemy, the Wizard replied.

You are a liar.

You must not fight me. I am—the Wizard repeated.

And on and on, more intense, more savage with each exchange.

In time Blade sensed that his own thoughts were coming more slowly and knew he would have to find some new defense. So he shifted to problems in calculus. He'd always been competent rather than brilliant at mathematics. To do any problem in calculus in his head took total concentration. As the numbers began to dance across his mental vision, he felt the Wizard driven back—and also felt his growing anger.

In another moment, Blade could no longer read the thoughts the Wizard was using to try breaking through his own mental smokescreen of equations. Perhaps he was winning, or at least holding his own. He decided to test the idea. He thought of taking a step backward, then of raising both hands high over his head and lowering them. His muscles told him that his legs and his arms were obeying his mind. His mind and body were still his own, not the Wizard's.

The moment's break in Blade's mental defenses gave the Wizard his chance for a physical act. He took two swift steps forward, one arm shot out, and a heavy hand pressed itself against Blade's temple.

Blade jerked his mind back to the equations, but he felt the attack against him double its strength. He still read anger in that attack, but also curiosity. A mind as hard to penetrate and control as Blade's was clearly something new and mysterious for the Wizard.

That might be good news, if it kept the Wizard reluctant to kill him. It would also make the Wizard more determined

73

than ever to break into his mind and find out what made it tick! This fight wasn't going to be over for a long time.

Suddenly the Wizard hurled his thoughts with total concentration and tremendous force at Blade. Blade's defenses started to collapse, slowly but inevitably, like a falling wall. He knew they were collapsing, knew that the Wizard was about to enter his mind. Images of London, of the computer room, of his apartment flashed across his mental vision instead of the equations.

This time it was Blade's chance to use his body. With all the willpower he had left, Blade forced his right arm into movement. His hand closed around the hilt of the Wizard's dagger and plucked it from the sash. He raised the sharp steel, holding it well out to one side so the Wizard could not grab it easily. Then he concentrated totally on an image of himself and the Wizard lying on the floor. The Wizard's throat gaped open, while Blade lay with the dagger buried up to the hilt in his chest. Both were as lifeless as the blood-drenched stone under them.

The Wizard jerked his hand away from Blade's temple as if it had suddenly turned red-hot and leaped backward. He made no effort to grab the dagger. Instead he dropped into a wrestler's crouch and raised one hand to send the Wolves into action.

The Wolves took two steps forward. Then Blade raised the dagger and held it with the point almost touching the bare skin of his chest. At the same time he formed in his mind another image—his dead body sprawled on the floor, with the Wizard and the Wolves standing around it, gaping helplessly.

The Wolves took another step forward. Blade gulped in air, realized that he'd bitten his lips hard enough to draw blood, and forced out words.

"No," he said. "No, Wizard. Stop them where they are, or you'll never get anything from me. I can be dead long before they reach me."

The Wizard stiffened for a moment, then nodded. The hand went up again and the Wolves stopped. The Wizard straightened, his eyes narrowed, and Blade knew he was gathering his thoughts for another mental attack.

"No," said Blade again. "Stay out of my mind, too. I don't like that, any more than I like the Wolves. Leave me unharmed and free, both in mind and body, or see me dead in front of you."

74

"You wouldn't dare," was the thought that came clearly from the Wizard.

Don't risk it, was Blade's reply. *It seems that I have something you value. You will not get it or anything else if I die, and I will die if you touch either my body or my mind again. Do not doubt this for a moment.*

Blade was not bluffing. Death *might* be worse than whatever the Wizard had in store for him, but he doubted it. In any case, he could do nothing to affect the Wizard's behavior once he lost control of his mind. He couldn't risk leaving himself at the man's mercy.

It was literally and brutally a case of liberty or death.

The two men stood glaring at each other for a minute that seemed like an hour. Neither moved an inch, or paid any attention to the five Wolves. The men were blinking and shuffling their steel-shod feet, certain that something was badly wrong, equally certain they didn't know what it was or what they should do.

Then the Wizard let his breath out in a long sigh and lowered his gaze to the floor. His hands dropped to his sides and Blade noticed that they were visibly shaking. His olive face had gone pale and sweaty, while his eyes blinked furiously.

At last he got control of himself and again met Blade's eyes.

"Who are you?" he rasped. "Who are you, Richard Blade? Where did you come from, and when did you come from?"

Blade found it hard not to gape stupidly at the Wizard. The questions made no sense at all. He wondered if the strain of the mental duel might not have temporarily muddled the Wizard's mind.

"Do you *know* who you are?" said the Wizard. "Do you remember, or have you forgotten?" He was impatient, but there was also a pleading note in his voice. Blade could no longer doubt that this was a desperate man in front of him— but desperate about *what?* The man's questions still made no sense.

"Who are *you?*" he shot back. "Tell me, and then I will know if it is safe to tell you who I am." The Wizard's face twisted, but Blade raised the dagger again. The Wizard swallowed, then took a deep breath.

"I am Bernardo Sembruzo, Conde di Pietroverde," he said. "I was a nobleman of Milan and a captain in the service of the Visconti. I fought against Florence. After the death of the great Gian Galeazzo, I retired to my estates. There I explored the secrets of the world around us and also of the world within our minds. I explored too deeply, and one day I passed from my castle to—here, Rentoro."

The Wizard said all this without stopping for breath. Now he gulped in air and repeated, "Where did you come from, Richard Blade, and when did you come from there? I came from my castle, north of Milan, in the Christian year 1410. When did you leave Earth, Blade, and come to Rentoro?"

Chapter 13

For a moment Blade could not have said a single coherent
word to save his life. He clamped his mouth firmly shut to
keep it from hanging helplessly open. Then he found he had
to close his eyes, shutting out the world and the man facing
him so he could organize his thoughts.

*This man says that he traveled across the Dimensions from
Renaissance Italy.*

That thought might have been written in giant fiery letters
across Blade's mental vision. It was quickly followed by other
thoughts, equally clear, equally insistent.

*This is the most astonishing claim I have ever heard any
human being make about himself. Do I believe it?*

*Why should he be lying? In fact, how could he lie? He has
mentioned too many places, names, and dates not to have
had some contact with Home Dimension. How do you explain it otherwise?*

Don't try to explain it. Let the Wizard do the explaining.

How?

You know there is only one way.

Dangerous.

*No matter how dangerous it is, you must use it. You can-
not let this man slip away. Not if he can cross into Dimension X by the power of his mind alone.*

"Too bloody right," muttered Blade, his lips at last able to
form words. He looked at the Wizard. "Bernardo Sembruzo"
was staring at him, eyes narrowed, hands clasped behind his
back. His dark face was twisted into a frown.

At last the Wizard took a deep breath and forced a thin
smile on to his face. "I see that you do not believe I am telling the truth. No, no, I am not trying to enter your mind
again. You have shown me that would not be wise and I have
some pride in my wisdom. What you think of me is written
large upon your face."

Blade was able to return the smile. "I can say the same thing about you. It is very easy to hear in your words and see on your face that you want something from me."

"Yes," said the Wizard, irritably. "I have said it several times. I want to know when you came from Earth to Rentoro, and from where?"

"Yes, but you want to know these things because you want my help. In fact, you want my help desperately. You want to know if I can help you return home."

The Wizard's face turned even paler than before and his lips tightened into an almost invisible line. Both hands rose, twisting into claws. Blade tightened his grip on the dagger, suspecting that the Wizard was about to leap at his throat, but almost certain his shot in the dark had gone home.

The moment passed. The Wizard's hands dropped back to his sides. He turned slowly to the five Wolves. "Leave, and do not return until I summon you. Chergin, give me your dagger." One of the Wolves handed his dagger to his master, who stuck it in his sash. The five Wolves clanked out of the room and the door slammed shut behind them. The Wizard turned back to Blade.

"You have guessed wisely. Does that mean you believe my story?"

"It does not."

"But—"

"My lord Wizard," said Blade briskly. "How much more time are we going to waste arguing like a couple of pimps in a cheap whorehouse? You interest me, even if you are not telling the truth. And if you are—"

"*I* interest *you?*" exploded the Wizard, his pride as nobleman, ruler of Rentoro, and explorer of the unknown violently pricked. "You dare—"

"Yes, I do," said Blade. "You seem to know that I have crossed the unknown, the way you say you have done. You should also know that a man who has done that will dare a great many things. I am no weakling."

The Wizard seemed to find that last remark wildly amusing. He threw back his head and laughed until the room was echoing and tears streamed down his face. "No, no certainly you are no weakling," he said at last. "What do you propose?"

Blade pointed to the floor. "Throw your dagger aside and lie on your back on the floor. I will kneel beside you. Raise your hand and place it on my head. Send your thoughts into my mind—thoughts of all you have seen and done, both in Italy and here in Rentoro. When I know you are telling the truth, I will think of what I have said and done, so that you may read my thoughts. That way I will know if you are lying. If you are—we shall see what happens. If not, you will have a chance to learn all you might wish to know about me."

The Wizard frowned. "I do not like being so vulnerable. If you chose to stab me as I lay—"

"Why should I do that? You have the sense not to risk killing a man who has traveled from Earth to Rentoro. Why should you think I am less sensible? Neither of us can really wish to kill the other unless he is a fool, and we are neither of us fools. No, I keep the dagger in order to kill myself, if you seek to control my mind. I will never let my mind be under your control. Accept that now and do not forget it. Also," Blade continued, "do not think you can simply turn your back on me and leave me here to starve for another week, until I am so feeble a child could overpower me. I will not permit that. If you leave this room without doing what I have proposed, I will be dead on the floor in the next moment—Is all of this clear? If it is, then why not act like the wise and brave man you are? You have much to gain if you go ahead, and much to lose if you do not."

Blade hoped he'd convinced the Wizard. Otherwise his last moments might be at hand, because he was absolutely certain that death would be preferable to letting the Wizard control his mind. He also hoped that he wouldn't have to argue like this every time he and the Wizard didn't see eye to eye!

The silence continued, until at last the Wizard's shoulders sagged slightly. He forced a smile on to his face, but there was no pleasure in his voice when he spoke.

"Very well, I see that I can expect nothing better from you. Your skill in arraying your arguments is as great as the skill of Sir John Hawkwood in arraying his men."

Blade remembered that Sir John Hawkwood had been an English soldier of fortune, the first of the great *condottieri* and the chief general of the city of Florence against the Visconti. He was being praised very highly indeed.

"Thank you, my lord count," said Blade, with a slight nod.

The sour mood seemed to leave the Wizard and his smile broadened. "Come, come. I think we need not waste more time in courtly exchanges. This is not the Palazzo Ducale in Milan." He drew his dagger, holding it by the point, and threw it to the far corner of the room. Then he lay down on the floor on his back. Blade knelt beside him.

"Are you ready, Blade?"

"I am."

The Wizard frowned in concentration, then raised his hand and pressed it against Blade's forehead. Blade held the dagger in both hands, the point an inch from his chest, ready to drive it in by pure reflex the moment he felt the Wizard seeking control of his mind. Their eyes met once again, briefly— then the room around them vanished in the sequence of images the Wizard was pouring into Blade's mind.

—A young knight, clearly the Wizard at nineteen or twenty, riding up and down the tilting yard, practicing with lance, sword, and shield.

—The same man, riding across green fields of waving grass, picking off birds with a small crossbow, his servants riding behind to pick them up.

—Grimmer scenes, many of them in rapid succession, of the wars in which the Visconti of Milan sought to weld northern Italy into a single kingdom under their rule. Pitched battles in the open field, ambushes by night, a tent where wounded men lay moaning in fever or screaming with pain as the surgeon set smashed bones and probed for arrowheads, the walls of Florence with their flaunted banners looming above the battlements. Finally the deathbed of Gian Galeazzo Visconti, and the collapse of all the Visconti hopes to be kings in Italy.

—A small but strong castle, perched on a rocky spur, with vineyards, olive orchards, and fields of grain spreading around it.

—A chamber, high in the tower of the castle, where the Wizard, now a man with his face lined and gray showing at his temples, read scrolls, mixed fuming chemicals, sat in meditation or trances, slowly grew thin and hollow-eyed with the strain of his explorations of the unknown.

—A nightmare of swirling, dancing colors and images, as the Wizard's mind twisted itself, creating a whole new set of senses, so that Home Dimension slipped away.

—The Wizard awakening in a field in Rentoro, within sight of a hill Blade recognized as the one where the castle now stood. The Wizard was unarmed, but he was fully clothed.

80

—The people drifting out from the nearest town to start work on the great castle. Some came with smiling or at least curious faces. Others came with the slow tread and the blank faces of zombies.

On and on, image after image, each image confirming both the Wizard's own tales and everything Blade had heard from Lorya. Blade saw the training of the Wolves, the burning of rebellious towns, the hanging of rebels, the last great battle outside the walls of Morina. He saw a courtyard and a line of Wolves galloping across it, to pass between two glowing objects lying on the ground and vanish into thin air.

He saw a room in the castle, with row after row of great glass bowls on carved wooden shelves. He saw the Wizard take down one of the glass bowls, place it on the floor in front of him, then comtemplate it. An image sprang into life inside the bowl—and Blade recognized the walls of Dodini.

He saw another room, where the Wizard sprawled on a silk-draped couch, wearing only red silk trousers and a dagger, waited on hand and foot by lovely young women who wore nothing at all.

He saw what seemed to be the shaft of a mine, where gaunt men with tangled hair and beards slaved to move great chunks of some crystalline substance onto hoists or into carts. Other men with wolf badges watched over the miners, urging them on with long iron-tipped whips.

At last the Wizard stopped sending images, and Blade saw no more. He stood up and stepped back on legs that shook slightly. He was breathing hard and sweating, as if he'd just run several miles with man-eating tigers at his heels.

Bernardo Sembruzo, Conde di Pietroverde, the Wizard of Rentoro, was everything his own words and the legends of Rentoro said he was. He was a telepath who could reach, read, and control other minds. He was a scientist who'd discovered some form of matter transmission. He was the discoverer of a method of traveling into Dimension X by the unaided power of the human mind.

He was, in short, the single most important human being alive in any Dimension Blade knew.

He was also an Italian Renaissance nobleman, who was using all these vast gifts to rule Rentoro like an Italian Renaissance tyrant. This did not diminish his gifts. It did greatly increase the danger of dealing with him.

Blade shook his head furiously, like a man surrounded by

a swarm of buzzing, whining insects. Here in the Wizard's castle he'd discovered mysteries not only far beyond what he'd expected, but far beyond what he would have believed possible. Hunger, fatigue, and astonishment slowed his thoughts, but he forced them into motion. What next? Find out exactly what the Wizard must know from you, came the answer.

Blade licked dry lips. "I believe you now. I have learned enough from you. What do you want to know from me?"

The Wizard shrugged. "The same as I have been asking. Where do you come from, when did you leave it for Rentoro, and how did you get here?"

"You will not need to enter my mind for any of this?"

"Not if you tell me freely."

That was reasonable enough, so Blade told the Wizard of his own Home Dimension, of Lord Leighton and J, of the computer and his journey to Rentoro. As he spoke, he thought he saw the Wizard's face set into a hard mask and his shoulders sag again.

When Blade was finished, the Wizard sighed. "So I thought it was with you," he said. "I entered your mind briefly, while you lay asleep with the woman. I saw pictures of much of what you have just described, but they were confused, as is often the case in the mind of a sleeping man. I could not understand, but I would not risk waking you and warning you. I learned your name, I learned that you had come to Rentoro from some other world, and that you would seek me out. That was enough, for the moment."

"I see," said Blade. That explained the strange dreams, the night after he'd rescued Lorya and fled with her from Dodini.

"Now I learn that you have come to me from England, but an England more than five hundred years in the future of my Milan. You have come not by the powers of your own mind, although those powers are great, but by a vast mechanical device I do not understand. What I do understand, though, is that you seem to offer me no way home. You could perhaps help me cross the Dimensions to your time and home, but not to cross time to my castle and my own people." The Wizard's voice was level and expressionless. Only the hands, clenched until the knuckles stood out white, revealed his anguish.

Blade knew that he had to say something encouraging, that would convince the Wizard of his value. He also knew that

82

he had to choose his words very carefully. In disappointment or in anger, the Wizard could have him killed with no more trouble than swatting a fly.

"We do not know that we cannot travel in time," he said slowly. "In fact, we have never tried. We have sought to cross the Dimensions, not to explore our own past. If you were to return with me to the England of my time, perhaps you will be able to return from there to your own time and place. Certainly you will have a better chance of doing so than if you stay here in Rentoro, where you have no chance at all."

"That is true enough," said the Wizard. "I have sought the way back many times, but I have yet to find it."

It occurred to Blade that his next question might anger the Wizard. Still, he had to know just how valuable he might be to the Wizard, and therefore how much bargaining power he had. *How badly did the Wizard want to go home?* This could be a matter of life or death.

"Why do you want to go home at all?" Blade asked quietly. "It seems to me that you have everything here any man could want or hope to gain. The Visconti did not become kings, but you certainly have."

"One could perhaps say that," said the Wizard, even more quietly. "Indeed, I am a king. I am also alone. Have you ever been alone, Richard Blade, so alone that you can understand what I am trying to say?"

Blade did not hesitate before replying. He could not mistake the sincerity—and the utter loneliness—in the Wizard's voice. It would be safe to risk anything, even his life, on the Wizard's need for his help. He nodded.

"I understand—friend Bernardo."

"That is good—friend Richard."

They shook hands. Then the Wizard opened the door and shouted into the hall outside, "Ho! Bring food and clothing for Richard Blade. At once!"

The Wizard stood by the door until his servants appeared with a chamber robe and a meal of bread, cheese, hot soup, and wine for Blade. Blade ate and drank cautiously, to avoid straining his stomach after the long fast. At last the meal was over and the Wizard silently followed his servants out of the room, leaving Blade alone.

Blade leaned back against the heaped pillows on the bed and ran the scene just finished through his mind again. Now he had a better idea of what he faced and the prospect would have appalled him if it hadn't been so enormously exciting.

Leighton and J would be more than happy to send the Wizard back to Renaissance Italy, if they could. But first they would insist on his revealing all the secrets of his paranormal powers. Examined by competent scientists, the Wizard might reveal the secret of traveling between the Dimensions by sheer mental power.

Then Dimension X would lie open to Britain, and all at once the Project would have justified itself ten times over. Lord Leighton might grumble about his magnificent computer being made obsolete, but he was too good a scientist to protest seriously.

There was going to be much more talking with the Wizard before anything happened, though. The man had raised almost as many questions as he'd answered. One in particular stood out.

In all his words and thoughts, the Wizard had shown only one man, himself, doing everything that must have been done by several generations of Wizards. He seemed to think he was the same man who'd served in the armies of the Visconti, still alive and ruling in Rentoro after more than a century.

Was the Wizard simply mad—at least on that one point?

Had his ancestors passed on their memories to him by telepathy, so that he knew everything they'd seen and done as if he'd done it himself? Perhaps there had been four or five Wizards, but only one mind and only one set of memories, now in its fourth or fifth body?

Or could it be that the Wizard *was* just one man? In that case he would be well into his second century, although he looked no more than thirty-five. Did the powers of his mind extend to retarding the aging process? This seemed the most fantastic notion of all, but was it much less fantastic than the existence of the Wizard in the first place?

Blade laughed. His exploration of the mysteries of the Wizard of Rentoro was not over. In fact, it had just begun.

Chapter 14

Blade spent the next three days resting, exercising, and eating five meals a day to restore his strength. He half expected that by the time he was back in fighting trim, the Wizard might have changed his mind about their alliance. Whether or not the Wizard was actually a man from the Italian Renaissance, he seemed to think like one. That meant double-edged words and open treachery would be a normal part of his life. Blade knew he had to rely as much as possible on his own strength and skill, and as little as possible on the Wizard's friendship.

In fact, the Wizard kept every promise he'd made, then made a few more and kept those as well. Bernardo Sembruzo (or Bernardo Sembruzo's great-grandson) seemed more and more a man of the Renaissance as Blade came to know him better. He ruled as a tyrant, was more than capable of treachery, and had a wide streak of sadistic cruelty in him. He was also brilliant, cultivated, and extraordinarily charming when he chose to be. In short, a man of fascinating (even if sometimes alarming) contradictions.

The Wolves were another matter. Few of them had any charm or knowledge of anything except fighting. They were nothing more than the faithful servants of a tyrant. Blade did not regret the ones he'd killed, and sometimes hoped for a chance to kill a few more.

He soon forgot about the Wolves. Indeed, he soon forgot to wonder whether the Wizard was immortal or a madman. Whoever he was, the man had amazing powers and showed Blade one amazing sight after another.

The Wizard's knowledge of everything that went on in Rentoro was easily explained after he showed Blade the glass balls on shelves in the Great Hall of the castle. They were actually balls of a sort of crystal. The Wizard or one of his dozen trained and trusted assistants would rest their hands on one of the balls and concentrate. There would be a milky swirling within the ball, and then a scene would flash into view, every detail and movement shown perfectly. Each ball was "tuned" to a particular city or town. By a simple exercise of will, the man at the view-ball could send his vision anywhere in the city or town. He could see anything—wedding nights, births and deaths, or the hatching of plots against the Wizard. He could also see the messages of the Wizard's allies and spies.

It appeared that the Wizard could send thought messages to trained men—spies or Wolf leaders—anywhere in Rentoro. He could not so easily receive messages or read minds over long distances. His spies either sent their reports to the view-balls, or rode in person to his castle and let him hear their words and thoughts.

Blade found it oddly consoling that the Wizard could not do everything, or at least wouldn't admit to doing everything.

Blade was getting used to the idea of dealing with a telepathic genius. He was glad he wouldn't have to deal with an out and out superman!

The crystal had another use beside giving the Wizard his magical, all-seeing eyes. In a slightly different form, it created the "sky-bridges"—the teleportation links that hurled the Wolves from one end of Rentoro to another in the space of a single breath.

The sky-bridge was simple enough, once Blade got used to the idea that it existed at all. A selected crystal was carefully divided into four precisely equal components. One pair was placed somewhere in the castle, the other near a city or town. When activated by the Wizard or one of his assistants, the four pieces together formed a sky-bridge. Then the Wolves could ride or march between the two crystals at the castle end, appear between the other pair, and descend on the city or town.

There were more than sixty sky-bridges. There was one for each large city or town in Rentoro, and as many more scattered about the country, carefully hidden. Among them, the sixty let the Wizard put down a force of Wolves, ready for action, close to any place in Rentoro, within an hour of giving the order. Of the total of six thousand Wolves, two hundred were always in armor, their heudas saddled and their weapons ready at hand. They were the first, and if more were needed all the rest of the Wolves could follow within a day.

None of it would have made any sense to Blade, if he hadn't seen it in action with his own eyes. He could not doubt it, and therefore had to force his sometimes half-numb mind to understand it. Certainly it explained why the Wolves were invincible. If all the fighting men of Rentoro gathered into a single army, they would outnumber the Wolves five or six to one. The problem lay in gathering them, before the Wizard could detect them and the Wolves could strike. So far no one in Rentoro had ever solved that problem, so the Wizard's rule remained unbroken after more than a century.

The Wizard knew very well that he had to keep the sky-bridges a closely guarded secret from the Rentorans. "It is the most vital link in the chain that holds up my power," he said. "It is also the weakest. If the Rentorans knew of the crystals at the far end of each bridge, they would search high and low. Certainly they would find and destroy many, perhaps most. Then I would be thrown back into the castle, to stand or die. The sky-bridges must be made of a perfect crystal, cut with great art and tuned with great skill. So if the sky-bridges fell down, it would be hard to replace them before the Rentorans cast aside their fear of the Wolves and rose against me."

"Is that why your spies must ride to the castle to make their reports?" asked Blade.

"Yes. They do not know of the sky-bridges, and they will never be allowed to learn. They must live among the Rentorans, and sooner or later one who knew would have the secret tortured out of him. The Wolves, on the other hand, never spend a single night in any town or city. They never allow themselves to be captured, and I have also hypnotized each one so that he would go mad if anyone asked him about the sky-bridges."

Once more, the Wizard seemed to have laid out an impressive defense in depth. Not surprising, considering the importance of what he was defending. Blade wondered if the Wizard had a map showing all the outer crystals of the sky-bridges. He stopped wondering. If the map existed at all outside the Wizard's own mind, there was no chance of his allowing Blade to see it and no point in Blade's even asking.

There was also no point in his sending a message to Lorya, waiting in Peloff. Now that he knew the Wizard's secrets, the Wizard would be very careful about letting Blade communicate with the outside world. Trying to reassure Lorya could arouse the Wizard's suspicions and lead to her death. Blade realized he would just have to remain silent, and hope Lorya would get safely out of Peloff when the agreed-on waiting period came to an end.

What the Wizard did with the crystals was marvelous. How he got them in the first place was almost depressingly ordinary. They came out of a secret mine in the mountains that formed the eastern border of Rentoro. There was no route to the mines from the plains below. The Wizard and the Wolves who guarded the mine went back and forth through a sky-bridge. The slaves they escorted were the young men taken from the cities and towns of Rentoro, and they never left the mine alive.

The Wizard took Blade to the mine once. Blade saw the same things he'd seen in the Wizard's thoughts—the shafts and tunnels, the pits, the hoists and pulleys, and the gaunt, hairy men everywhere. He also saw the hunted, savage look in the men's eyes, and the comparative handful of Wolves who guarded them.

"How many men does the mine need?"

"I only need a few hundred," said the Wizard. "But there are more than a thousand here now, and sometimes there are even more. I take more young men than I need, to remind the people that I rule in Rentoro. It is also a good punishment for rebels. Not even the strongest man can last for more than a year in the crystal mine." The look in the Wizard's eyes as he spoke the last words turned Blade's stomach. The Wizard might not be mad, but certainly the streak of sadistic cruelty in him was not fully under control. Taking him back to Home Dimension was still absolutely necessary, but would it be absolutely safe? Blade couldn't help wondering.

Compared to the view-balls and the sky-bridges, even compared to the crystal mine, the castle was almost commonplace. It had everthing needed for the Wizard's comfort or luxury, everything an Italian Renaissance nobleman would have allowed himself, if he'd been in a position to indulge every whim. There was a cellar full of barrels of wine, there was a library of scrolls and illuminated books richly bound in leather, there was a roomful of jewels and another of fine weapons and armor. There was a kitchen that could turn out delicate sauces or roast a whole ox, and piles of silver and gold dishes for serving anything the kitchen turned out. There was a state apartment, with a jeweled bed hung with silk curtains embroidered in pearls and golden thread. There was luxury to wallow in, until Blade found himself surprised that the Wizard wasn't a bloated hulk of flesh instead of a hard-muscled fighting man. Only an iron will could have kept him from decaying—but then, any man who could rule as the Wizard did had enough willpower to do almost anything.

All this luxury was for the Wizard himself. There was more for those who served him. The dozen assistants he'd trained each had a luxurious apartment of their own. The Wolves had their barracks, warm, snug, and comfortable. The craftsmen, the servants, the house guards, even the farm laborers had their own quarters and never went short of food or clothing.

Then there were the women. Some were slaves, some were free servants. All the young ones were also concubines—for the Wizard, for his assistants, for the Wolves, for the male servants and laborers. Since nature was allowed to take its course, they were also the mothers of future Wolves, concubines, and laborers.

The Wizard was not only the distant tyrant who ruled over Rentoro. He was also the personal and quite absolute ruler of a community of thousands of men and women. Every one of them existed to serve him and his rule, and most of them worshipped or feared him as if he was very nearly a god.

It was a situation that would have corrupted a saint, and there was very little saintliness in Bernardo Sembruzo. Blade didn't like the Wizard's streak of self-indulgent cruelty any better, but he gradually came to understand it.

At first Blade wasn't sure what to do about the women. It was impossible to ignore them. Most of those who waited on him and the Wizard were beautiful. None of them wore very much, and some of them wore nothing at all except subtle and exciting perfumes. Blade wondered if he was supposed to keep his hands off them, and if so, how long he would be able to do so. In some things, Richard Blade was no more of a saint than Bernardo Sembruzo.

The Wizard was not long in realizing Blade's doubts, and in cheerfully inviting him to make free with the women. "After all," he said, "you have all my secrets. Why should you not have a few of my women as well? You are the only ally and the only true friend I have ever had since I came to Rentoro, and one of the few I have ever had. Only you have been able to offer me a road home."

"I have offered a hope of one," said Blade quietly. "I would rather you did not depend too much on that hope. I will not promise that either or both of us will safely reach England, or that my friends can send you back to your own land and time from there."

"All at once you seem very doubtful of your success," said the Wizard, his eyes narrowing.

"I am no more doubtful of my success than I was before," said Blade. "What I doubt is my own safety, if you hope for too much and then are disappointed."

"Richard, my friend, that is an unworthy thought between men of gentle birth. You should be ashamed of it."

"I would be more ashamed to walk blindly to my death, when a few words could make us understand each other clearly. Such foolish carelessness is not for men of gentle birth, either."

"Perhaps not. Very well—on my honor I swear that if we cannot return to your England, no harm will come to you. Indeed, you shall continue at my right hand, and by my friend and comrade in the ruling of Rentoro. Though we shall be alone, yet we shall have no small pleasure in our lives from that rule."

"I can ask nothing more," said Blade. Indeed, he could not, or at least he didn't care to try. For all the friendship the Wizard had shown him, he was still as vulnerable as ever to the man's whims. The less the Wizard was provoked, the better.

Chapter 15

Although the Wizard gave Blade free run of the women of the castle, nothing came of it for a while except a certain amount of pleasure. Even that was limited, at least from Blade's point of view. The Wizard's women were so desperate in their eagerness to please that the mere possibility of angering Blade made them shiver with fright and even burst into tears. Or was it the Wizard's displeasure they feared, for not doing their best for their master's sworn friend and comrade? All the women showed the signs of years of obedience to the Wizard's whims and temper. A few of them showed fresh bruises from the Wizard's more violent moments. After a while, none of them could really please Blade.

In spite of the odds against him, he tried asking some of the women questions about the Wizard's affairs. A few of them answered, but none of them told him anything new and important. Others seemed so frightened at his questions that he abandoned the effort before the women were driven to telling the Wizard.

Blade did learn one thing from the women. The Wizard hadn't aged visibly during the time that any of the women had been serving in the castle. Still, that was no more than ten years, and a man who kept himself in good shape and dyed his hair and beard might very well not change. Blade was no nearer finding out if the Wizard was immortal, mad, or simply shared his ancestors' memories.

In any case, it really did not matter that much. Even if the present Wizard of Rentoro was not the same man as the one who'd traveled across the Dimensions, he was certainly a telepath and the master of the view-balls and sky-bridges. He could also teach many of his skills to other men. This was more than enough to make bringing him back to Home Dimension a monumental victory for Project Dimension X and for Britain. Blade saw no need to change any of his plans.

One evening over dinner he casually remarked that he found some of the women of the castle "a boring lot."

"I see that you've beaten obedience into them," Blade continued, "but you also seem to have beaten the spirit out of them."

The Wizard shrugged. "The wise ones, I didn't have to beat. They knew or could guess what I wanted from the first. But others—yes, I did have to use the stick a trifle. A few I even had to throw to the Wolves for a night or two. That cured them." A satisfied smile spread across the Wizard's face. "I take it you'd prefer someone with—more life, shall we say?"

"You might say that," said Blade.

"I think that can be arranged," said the Wizard. "There's one lady I have here I was never able to cure. Even throwing her to the Wolves just made her go astray in her wits. I've given up on her, but if you want to try?"

"I'll think about it," said Blade. "Why do you keep her around, if she's so hard to tame?" The Wizard seldom kept the useless or the disobedient around his castle or in his service at all.

"I wouldn't, except that she's a high noble of Morina. Sister to the ruling duke, in fact, and highly thought of by the people. Her brother was more than happy to send her to me, but the Morinans weren't happy to see her go. I've got to keep her around until she dies a natural death, otherwise the city will be in an uproar. I'd have to send in the Wolves and make such a shambles I'd get no taxes out of the place for two years.

"By all means try her, if you're interested. If you get her down it might improve her disposition. Don't kill her, but otherwise—" The Wizard waved a casual hand.

Blade wished he could hit the Wizard over the head and lock him in a closet until the time came to return to Home Dimension. Enduring the man's whims for the sake of their "friendship" was becoming something of a strain. Now he was being invited—indeed, practically ordered—to rape a madwoman. He should have kept his mouth shut about the castle's women!

"Very well," Blade said. "I'll see about paying her a visit tomorrow."

"Good. I'll leave the necessary orders with the guards. And now—more wine?"

The Morinan lady's room was high up in one of the towers, where she could get a reasonable amount of sunlight and fresh air. This had nothing to do with kindness—the Wizard would have done as much for a prize sow that he had to keep in good health.

Two of the house guards were on duty outside the room when Blade arrived. One of them unlocked the iron-bound door and held it slightly ajar.

"Now, 'member, lord—any trouble, gi' us a shout—we be in straight."

"Don't worry," said Blade. "I'm sure I'm big enough to handle her." The guards caught his double meaning and were still laughing as he slipped into the room.

It was circular, twenty feet across, eight feet high, and whitewashed so heavily Blade felt as if he'd stepped inside a wedding cake. It was a moment before he noticed the low bed on the far side of the room, under the barred window. It was another moment before he noticed the woman in the stained white robe, lying face down on the bed.

As Blade stepped toward the bed, the woman rolled over in a swirl of silk and pale legs, then raised her head to look at Blade. Her eyes were enormous, staring wildly without understanding, and with huge dark circles under them. Her blonde hair was a tangled mess, dark and stiff with grime. She laughed, a low bubbling sound deep in her throat that made Blade's flesh crawl and nearly made him turn around and leave the room much faster than he'd come in. She raised a thin hand to point at him, a shaking hand with black circles under untrimmed fingernails. She laughed again, and then she swung her legs off the bed, sprang to her feet, and came toward Blade.

Blade forced himself to stand and meet the woman's eyes as she came at him. As he got a better look at her, he realized that she was beautiful, or at least would have been, except for the look in her eyes and her unhealthy thinness. Pale, freckled skin was stretched too tightly over fine bones, and what should have been the generous curves of breast, hip, and thigh were shrunken and flattened. She looked as if she hadn't eaten regularly for months or years.

Then her hands clawed at Blade's shoulders until her fingernails sank through his silk shirt into his flesh. He gripped her arms, trying to control her, but she broke free and stepped back just out of his reach. Her hands made another quick dart, this time to grip her robe at the level of her knees. Before Blade could move or speak, she jerked the robe over her head and flung it away from her so violently that it flew clear across the room.

Certainly the beauty was there, as if asleep under that pale skin showing too many bones. The breasts rose in a proud challenge, the hips and thighs curved gracefully even now, the long legs held both power and elegance. She tossed her head, and Blade wished her hair was clean, loose, and flowing, so he could see it swirl about her high cheekbones and the long, graceful throat. Then she was coming toward him again. There was still a madness in her eyes, but it was a madness of desire, and Blade no longer feared that his own manhood would collapse at the woman's touch.

She went down on her knees before him, her hands tore the seams of his hose, and her lips descended on his bared flesh. They worked upon him until desire was almost pain, and his hands were clutched in her hair, gripping her as if releasing her would release his own hold on life. She stood, and her hands clawed his shirt from his chest and shoulders. Then she gripped both his hands and dragged him toward the bed.

Blade still wore his hose as they lay down on the bed, and he wore them as he thrust deep into the woman. After that it did not matter, for he wouldn't have noticed or cared if he'd been wearing a full suit of plate armor, as long as the woman was there and he was in her.

Blade couldn't have imagined a joining like this before, and he could never describe it afterward. There were no words to do justice to the mixture of pleasure, amazement, and doubt. All he knew was that his joining—he would never call it a lovemaking—was at the same time one of the most exciting and one of the most terrible experiences of his life. He was aware of the woman's body and the incredible joy it was giving him and taking from him. He was just as aware of the ruined mind within that body, and what this joining might do to it or for it.

At last the peak came for both of them, and with terrible violence. Blade found the strength to lie beside the woman and the will to keep his arms protectively about her. He would not simply jump up and leave her lying here, whatever she might do next. He wasn't going to come here again, either. That might offend the Wizard, but his mind was made up. He

94

would look for some excuse that would satisfy the Wizard, but if he couldn't find one, then—

As Blade's thoughts turned to making up a tale for the Wizard, he became aware that the woman was shifting her position, so that her lips were against his left ear. Then those lips were moving, and in another moment he could make out words, in a whisper so faint they would have been lost a foot away.

"Thank you," the woman was saying. "I could not hope that you would do as well, when I had to keep up my play-acting. It is good acting, for it has confused the Wizard himself. I feared it might also confuse you. Now—let us talk, and swiftly. There is much to say, and not much time for saying it."

"You—" said Blade, then broke off as he realized why the woman was whispering so close to his ear. The room doubtless had evesdroppers listening for whatever was said within it.

"Yes," she said. "They listen to know if I am truly mad, and they must hear nothing to make them doubt. That would be danger for me, perhaps even for you. Lie where you are and listen. They say you are the Wizard's trusted friend and ally, who has penetrated all his secrets as no man has ever done before. I am Serana Zotair of Morina, who would free my people from the Wizard, and I am as sane as you are. Perhaps saner, if you are truly a friend of the Wizard."

Blade listened, curious, fascinated, excited, and hardly suspicious or surprised at all. Why should she lie? As for being surprised, Blade was past that now. in this mad Dimension, he would not have been particularly surprised if she'd told him she was the Empress of Japan!

She was alone here in the castle, she said, and she had few supporters of her plans even in her native Morina. There were many who hated the Wizard, but few willing to risk the fate he dealt out to his enemies.

She had not planned to become the Wizard's prisoner. That *would* have been the act of a madwoman. Then her brother conceived of showing his loyalty to the Wizard and getting rid of her by sending her to the castle. She could not ignore the opportunity this offered for digging out the Wizard's secrets.

Blade would know, she said, what she'd endured during the past two years. The Wizard would have told him of the beatings, the brutality from the Wolves, the confinement. Then there was the endless strain of seeming to be mad, a grim battle that at times had almost driven her into real madness. She'd endured it all, and for nothing. The Wolves had knowledge of the Wizard's secrets, but never spoke of them in her presence. The household guards and servants spoke freely, but they knew nothing.

Now Blade had come. He could make it all worthwhile, if he chose to help her. She could neither promise nor threaten anything if he didn't help her. She could only pray that what he knew of the Wizard would tell him what he should do.

Perhaps she was foolish, trusting Blade, the Wizard's intimate friend. Certainly he was the best opportunity she'd ever had. Long before she had another one as good, she would have lost her sanity, if not her life. So what choice did she have?

At this point Blade shifted position, so that his lips were against Serana's ear. In a whisper as soft as hers, he said, "What makes you think I would *not* help you?" and squeezed her hand.

There was a very long silence, during which Blade held on to Serana's hand and she was obviously trying hard not to burst into tears. Then she rolled over, nuzzled at his cheek, and put her lips back against his ear.

There was not much more to tell and after a few more minutes Blade rose, pulled on his clothes, and left the room. He got rid of his escorts as fast as possible, not wanting to hear any more of their coarse jokes. He also wanted to be alone to think through his plans in the light of this new situation.

Fortunately, he couldn't see that many changes would be needed. He would be visiting Serana again, probably several times, but that wouldn't bother the Wizard. During those visits, he could tell the woman everything he'd learned—enough to let Morina lead a successful rebellion against the Wizard.

Such a rebellion might not be necessary, of course. If the Wizard returned to Home Dimension with Blade, his rule over Rentoro would come to an end naturally. His trained assistants and the Wolves might do their best for a few years, but they would go down sooner or later, whether Morina rebelled or not.

Yet he had to guard against failure. The techniques for getting other people back from Dimension X were uncertain, unreliable, hardly more than guesswork. There was a good chance Blade would end up back in London while the Wizard stayed in Rentoro. That would not only cost Home Dimension the Wizard's secrets, but leave Rentoro under his tyranny. Blade was determined to at least prevent the second, if he could not accomplish the first.

So Serana Zotair had to learn all the Wizard's secrets, carry them safely to Morina, and reveal them. Blade could tell her everything she needed to know, but getting her out of the castle was another problem.

"I think I see a way," he told her, on his third visit. "The Wizard thinks I am a learned man. I will say that I believe you will not be cured of your madness unless you are returned to Morina. I will say that you may even die, if you are not sent home for at least a few months. The Wizard does not want to have your death on his hands."

"No, and neither does Duke Efrim, my brother. He will keep me closely confined, though."

"Will you be able to send messages to your friends?"

"Yes. But will they do anything? They have not done so, in all the years there has been talk of a new rebellion. Some call themselves leaders in that rebellion, but they have done little enough leading."

"They may have done nothing because it seemed they would be throwing their lives away in vain. With all the Wizard's secrets in their hands, the odds will be much better."

"I hope they will see this as clearly as you do. Will you be coming with me to Morina?"

"The Wizard does sometimes let me leave the castle, but not without an escort of Wolves. You would be safer going alone. Go on pretending to be mad, but eat a little more and get some strength back. You may need it, after you reach Morina." Then there were no further words, only quick breathing and writhing flesh. They had to make love as if Serana was still mad. Blade was sorry they would never be able to do it with the tenderness and affection they both now felt and wanted.

There were dangers in the plan. He could not go with Serana, and only partly for the reason he gave. He had to stay in the castle, close to the Wizard, or throw away any chance of taking the man home with him. Serana would have to play a lone game in Morina, but that should be almost easy for her after what she'd done these past two years in the Wizard's castle.

Blade would also have to make sure the Wizard didn't try to read Serana's thoughts before letting her go. He obviously hadn't done so before, otherwise he would have known that she wasn't mad. Suppose he did so now? There would be hell to pay, for he would be almost certain to learn not only that Serana was quite sane but that Blade had told her all his secrets. Blade suspected the best thing to do in that case would be kill the Wizard and then try to get clear with Serana in the resulting uproar and confusion. It would be a very poor "best."

Blade mentally kept his fingers crossed, and as the days turned into weeks, he began to think his plan might work. Serana stayed as wild-eyed and incoherent as before, but slowly she put on flesh. The Wizard listened politely to Blade's proposal, seemed to suspect nothing, and said he would give his answer in a week or two. Blade could only hope he would make up his mind before the computer reached out to haul one or both of them back to Home Dimension. If the Wizard did decide to let Serana go, and did not probe her mind, everything should be simple.

Then all at once nothing was simple, because of the Wizard's lastest idea.

Chapter 16

Blade and the Wizard were sitting up late in the Wizard's private dining room. Blade reached for the silver wine jug on the low table between them. Then the Wizard spoke and Blade froze with his hand in midair.

"I think it will not be necessary to return Serana Zotair to Morina. In fact, it will not even be possible. In another few weeks there will be no Morina."

Blade forced himself not to sit up with a jerk, and leaned back in his chair. "Oh? What is going to happen to it?"

"Happen to it, Blade? *I* am going to happen to it. My Wolves and I. It will be destroyed, so that when I am gone from Rentoro the people will come to where Morina stood and remember me. It will be destroyed, its houses and even its walls cast down, and its people slain to the last graybeard and squalling infant."

"Certainly the Rentorans will not forget you, if that is your farewell to them," said Blade. "But isn't it a rather large task?"

"Not for all my Wolves striking together, with surprise and terror on their side. It will be a most unusual sort of terror, for it will be *mine*."

"Yours?" Blade was having trouble understanding the Wizard's cryptic references. He was having even more trouble keeping his face expressionless.

"Yes, mine. I shall cross the sky-bridge with my Wolves for the first time, and I shall send terror into the minds of all the people of Morina. They will be an interesting sight, when they find my terror destroying their minds and my Wolves destroying their bodies."

Blade nodded politely, although "interesting" was not precisely the word he would have used. "Forgive me for raising this possibility again," he said. "What if we do not return to

England and it is your fate to remain here to the end of your life?"

"That will be a long time," said the Wizard. He shrugged. "If it is my fate to remain in Rentoro, the destruction of Morina will still do me no harm. The people will think that what I have done once, I can do again. They will be even more obedient than they have been, for they will be even more fearful than they have been. I will lose nothing, not even wealth, by destroying Morina. And if it is fate that we *both* remain here in Rentoro—" He broke off and looked at Blade, who tried even harder to seem perfectly calm. Then, "Richard, do you have sons—sons of your own loins?"

"Yes. I have left several behind me, during my travels."

The Wizard relaxed visibly. "That is good news—the very best news I could imagine." His voice was level as he continued. "You see, I have no children, neither sons nor daughters. I had none in Milan, and I have none here in Rentoro. I greatly fear there is no power in my loins to beget children. So I can have no heirs of my body, and I fear that all I have built in Rentoro will fall when I die. I would not have that happen. Too much of my life in Milan was wasted. I would not have it so here in Rentoro as well."

The Wizard smiled. "You wonder what I am trying to say, Blade? Well, I shall tell you in plain words. If it is our fate to both remain here in Rentoro, you shall be my heir. You shall be the next Wizard, and your sons shall come after you."

Once again, only the fact that he was getting used to surprises in this Dimension kept Blade from gaping. He returned the Wizard's smile. "I am vastly honored, and believe me when I say that I am grateful beyond words. But—I do not have your mental powers. Could I hope to rule Rentoro without them?"

"You do not have those powers," said the Wizard, in a gently chiding tone. "But you know those powers can be taught.

How else would my assistants be able to control the viewballs and the sky-bridges? I have only given my assistants some of the powers, but to you I would be prepared to give all of them. We would have many years, and you have a powerful mind. I would be very surprised if you could not learn to do everything I can do, and teach your sons in their turn."

"We may not have many years," said Blade. "Remember,

it is also possible that I may return to England while you stay here in Rentoro."

"I know that," said the Wizard impatiently. "I admit that would not make me happy. Still, something can be done about this. The most intelligent of the castle's women will be sent to your bed, and I shall teach the children you get on them. The best shall become my heir. And if we are fortunate, and do have years——"

"Yes?" Blade could not quite control his impatience. He wanted to learn the rest of the Wizard's plans, and then get out of here before he did anything to make the man suspicious. His self-control would not be enough to deceive a telepath much longer.

"If we have years, I shall pick out all the finest young women from Rentoro. I shall examine both the body and the mind of each one. The ten best shall all be sent to the castle, and all ten of them will become yours. You will get children on them, children strong in mind and body like their father and mothers. Then there will be heirs for both me and you, and the rule of the Wizards of Rentoro will never end!"

"You are an ambitious man, Bernardo."

"If I was not ambitious, would I be where I am today?"

There was no possible reply to that. Blade frowned in a pretense of concentration. "What about Serana Zotair? Do you plan to make her one of my harem?"

The Wizard shook his head. "Her mind is not strong enough to make her a worthy mother for your heirs. I have other plans for her." The Wizard smiled, but it was a smile Blade knew too well meant bad news.

"I shall have to examine her mind before I send the Wolves against Morina. If she is not helplessly mad, I shall take her with me when the city falls. It will be interesting to enter her mind and read her thoughts as she watches her city and her people die."

Blade's face was a mask and his voice was very level. "And if she is too mad to know what she is seeing?"

The Wizard shrugged. "Then there would be no pleasure for me in reading her thoughts. I will turn her over to the Wolves and they can do as they please with her."

"So I suppose I shall have to take as much pleasure as I can from her, these next few days?" said Blade, trying to smile.

"Yes," said the Wizard. "Unless you have a taste for corpses?" He laughed coarsely.

"Not I," said Blade. "Live ones only—the livelier the better."

"Shall we drink to that?" said the Wizard. He filled both cups and raised his. "To lively women!"

Blade drank and after that there was no more discussion of the fate of Morina. He found it easy to keep his face under control and after a few minutes was able to find an excuse for leaving.

Outside in the hall, he found he had to lean against the wall briefly before he could walk the rest of the way to his own rooms. Had the Wizard gone completely mad or was he just indulging himself more than usual?

It didn't matter. Mad or sane, the Wizard was perfectly capable of carrying out his plans for the destruction of Morina. Those plans had to be defeated. It would be better to defeat them without killing the Wizard himself, but if there was no other way—

If Morina could only be saved by killing the Wizard, then the Wizard would die. Blade's mind was made up on that. Twenty thousand people lived in and around Morina. He was not going to stand by and let them die, on the chance that he might be able to take the Wizard back to England with him.

He would also do his best to leave the Wizard alive.

The Wizard could teach all his skills and powers—or at least believed he could. If he could be brought back to Home Dimension, alive, sane, and ready to teach those who could learn—

It would be worth a good deal, even if not the lives of twenty thousand people. Blade's mind was made up on that, too.

The Wizard seemed to be in no hurry to launch the attack on Morina, so Blade chose not to arrange a special meeting with Serana. He wanted to avoid anything that might possibly arouse suspicion until he and Serana were safely inside the walls of Morina—or at least safely out of reach of the Wolves' swords and the Wizard's mental control.

So Blade visited Serana on schedule and they made love. It was becoming steadily harder for Serana to pretend to be mad while she was with Blade, and steadily harder for Blade to conceal the real affection he felt toward the woman. He knew both of them would be happy to drop the disguise.

They lay together afterward, in the usual wild tangle of sweaty limbs and tousled hair, and Blade told Serana the bad news. He felt her go rigid as a board against him and she was silent for a long time.

Then she said, her voice shaking slightly, "We must flee. At once."

"I know that. We must also begin the rebellion against the Wizard, whether your friends in Morina are ready or not."

"They can make themselves ready, once we tell them of what awaits the city if they do nothing."

"What about your brother?"

"He may not be our friend, even now. It is less likely that he will be our enemy. He is not evil enough to wish all his people slaughtered by the Wolves."

"You hope."

"What do you mean by that?"

"I mean that we must be on our guard against even your brother. We must be ready to deal with him as an enemy."

"Blade, you know I have no great love for my brother. Yet I must also think of the House of Zotair, and what my brother's death might mean for it."

"Think of Morina, then of your House."

"Blade, if my brother makes himself our enemy, then my hand will not tremble, any more than yours. Is that enough?"

"Yes."

Blade's hand drifted across Serana's breast. She shivered, then whispered, "How shall we flee?"

"We shall use one of the sky-bridges."

"How can we hope to do that? Does the Wizard trust you that much?"

"He has even let me use sky-bridges, as long as a few Wolves go with me. We can deal with them once the Wizard's assistant has activated the sky-bridge. Then we step between the crystals and pass beyond the Wizard's reach."

Serana let out a shuddering sigh. "Which sky-bridge do we use? Can we go straight to Morina? I would—"

Blade shook his head. "No, we go to Kassaro." That was a small town ten miles north of Morina. "Before we go, we destroy the castle end of the sky-bridge to Morina. After we reach Kassaro, we destroy the outer end of that sky-bridge. Then the Wolves will have to ride nearly twenty miles to reach the walls of Morina. They will lose surprise, face ambushes, and in general not have such an easy time of it."

"Morina cannot hold out against all the Wolves, even then."

"It won't have to. It only needs to hold out long enough for messages to go to all the other cities and towns in Rentoro. We will tell everyone the Wizard's secrets. Then every man, woman, and child will be seeking the outer ends of the sky-bridges and smashing the crystals. In a few weeks there will not be a sky-bridge left in Rentoro. Then the Wizard might still be able to see us gathering our armies, but he will not be able to send the Wolves against us."

"Not any faster than normal men can ride normal heudas, at any rate."

"No. Then the Wolves will be doomed. They will be outnumbered four or five to one, and they are not good enough to meet such odds. Not when the fighting men of Rentoro will have so much to avenge. It will be the end of the Wolves and the end of the Wizard's power in Rentoro." Blade was finding it hard to keep his voice down to a whisper. Excitement at the prospect of defeating the Wolves and breaking the Wizard's power swept through him.

"I pray that it may be so," murmured Serana. She was silent for a moment. "We go to Kassaro, you say, not to Peloff?"

Blade understood what Serana meant. "No. If Lorya is still alive and has obeyed my orders, she has long since left Peloff. If she is dead, we cannot help her. If she is alive but still in Peloff, she will have to take her chances."

"Poor chances they may be, against the Wizard and his Wolves."

"You think I don't know this?" Blade's whisper held an angry bite. "But Peloff is two weeks' ride from Morina. The Wolves would have many chances to catch us on the journey. If they could not do that, they could still ring Morina so thickly we could never get through to safety. They could also move into the city and have all your friends hanging dead from the walls before we came. It will be war—war to the death—the minute we lift a hand against one of the Wizard's people. Do you see that clearly?"

"Yes."

"Good. We have a little time to spare, since the Wizard does not seem ready to move against Morina at once. I think we can move the next time I visit you. Now, what I think is our best course is to—"

His voice faded until he was hardly more than moving his lips. Yet Serana understood, and a smile spread across her gaunt face.

After they'd talked, they made love again. Blade took extra care to seem harsh and brutal, and Serana screamed and howled like ten madwomen together.

At least this was the last time they'd have to put on such an act to deceive the Wizard's spies. With good luck, the next time they shared a bed, it would be in Morina. There was no point in thinking about what would happen if their luck was bad.

Chapter 17

Blade came to Serana after dark. They alternately made love and talked, until Blade was sure the Wizard must have gone to bed. He'd been boasting over dinner of how a new girl awaited him tonight, a peasant maid of sixteen. The Wizard took a great deal of pleasure with such new girls—so much pleasure that afterward he slept like a dead man, almost impossible to awaken and likely to fly into a rage at anyone who disturbed him. Tonight the castle servants, the castle guards, even the Wolf leaders would be reluctant to awaken their master for anything much short of the end of the world. That would make things a great deal easier for Blade and Serana.

In spite of this, Serana was so nervous that she spoke in jerky phrases, and Blade felt as if he was making love to a wooden statue. He was as relieved as she when the hourglass showed three hours had passed. If the Wizard wasn't dead to the world by now, he never would be.

"Ready?" he said, kissing her.

"Ready," she replied, between clenched teeth.

Blade threw back the blankets and started to climb out of bed. As he gave Serana a perfect target, she exploded into action. With a shrill scream, she lashed out with both feet and hands. She caught Blade in the groin, and now it was his turn to scream. With the horrible cry of a man who's just been castrated, he doubed up and toppled backward. As he fell, he managed to swing his head against the carved night table. He went limp and sprawled helpless on the floor, as Serana leaped out of the bed and started kicking at his ribs.

The next move was up to the guards outside the door, if they were watching. Blade's whole plan depended on their doing so, but he didn't think that was much of a gamble. This castle had the air of a place where everyone spied on everyone else. Besides, the guards wouldn't pass up a chance for some free entertainment, watching him and Serana together.

Serana went on kicking and screaming until Blade's ribs began to really hurt. He wondered if the guards would come before she had to go on to the next stage, clawing at him with her fingernails.

The door crashed open and two guards dashed in. Blade waited just long enough to be sure the hall outside was empty, then jerked one hand as a signal to Serana. She stopped kicking him and ran at the two guards, whimpering, clawing at her body, and tossing her head wildly. She made a frighteningly convincing madwoman, and she convinced the two guards. They came at her, one from each side, well apart, hands reaching out to grab her. They must have orders not to hurt her. As the guards came at her, Serana backed away. They followed her, until they were both within easy striking distance of Blade.

Suddenly Blade's limp body stiffened. Both feet shot out like a cannonball, to smash into the stomach of one guard. The man didn't scream, because he had no breath to scream with. He simply folded double, sat down in midair, then thumped to the floor. The other guard turned, realizing he'd walked into a trap. His mouth was opening to shout when Blade bounced to his feet and chopped the man across the throat. Instead of a shout, only gurgles and gasps came out as the guard choked to death. Blade turned to finish off his first victim, in time to see Serana stab the man to death with his own dagger.

Both guards were down, no alarm was up, and the hall outside lay empty before them. Blade shut the door, locked it from the inside, and stuffed a strip of blanket into the keyhole. Then he and Serana went to work.

Both guards were stripped naked and dumped into the bed. Blade arranged them so that they looked naturally asleep. Then he pulled the blankets over them and shoved pillows under their heads. Through the keyhole, no one who wasn't already suspicious would be likely to see anything unusual.

Then Serana pulled on one of the guards' outfits, from the skin out to the helmet and sword. Blade pulled on his own clothes and stuck the remaining sword and dagger in his belt. Once again, there would be no harm in having extra weapons ready to hand.

Serana smiled as she tightened the straps of her helmet. In

the helmet and baggy clothing, no one could tell that she was a woman. Her nervousness seemed to be completely gone. She doubled one hand into a fist and punched Blade lightly on one shoulder.

"All right, my mad love. Let's be on our way."

The hall outside was still empty. Blade pulled the strip of blanket out of the keyhole, locked the door behind them, and they moved out at a brisk trot. They didn't have to worry about arousing suspicion by hurrying. Blade normally moved about the castle at a pace that had his guards puffing to keep up with him. Tonight he was actually moving slower than usual, to avoid tiring Serana.

They passed through one hall after another, down one staircase after another, past one guard post after another. They met guards, servants, girls on their way to or from someone's bed, a cross section of the miniature city that was the Wizard's castle. No one paid any attention to them, except to give Blade a respectful greeting. No one knew exactly who or what he was, other than the Wizard's trusted friend and comrade, but for most of the people in the castle that was enough.

In all the years the castle had been standing, no one had ever seriously menaced it from within. There'd been servants' brawls, of course, and an occasional girl who objected to someone's rough lovemaking. That was all. No one had ever stalked through the halls of the castle, ready, willing, and able to kill anyone who crossed his path. No one would be expecting it, and people are slow to recognize what they do not expect. By the time anyone in the castle realized what was going on, Blade expected to be mounted and riding out of Kassaro.

The door from the citadel to the Wolves' barracks was guarded by a single Wolf. It needed no more. At any time of the day or night there were at least two thousand Wolves beyond the door, and who would want to get in or out unless they absolutely had to?

The Wolf raised a mail-gloved hand in salute as he saw Blade approaching. It was a slow and casual salute, almost defiant. The Wolves knew that Blade was a man who'd killed Wolves. They obeyed him out of loyalty to their master the Wizard, but they did not love any man who'd slain their comrades and still walked the earth alive and free.

"Greetings," said Blade. "It is my wish and the Wizard's

that I have an escort for a journey. It is short, so two Wolves will be enough."

"Shall I send to the stables as well?" asked the Wolf. That implied the question "Do you go by sky-bridge?" without mentioning the secret in the presence of one of the house guards.

Blade shook his head. The Wolf frowned. Blade could almost read the thoughts passing through his mind.

This sounds queer. But this man is the Wizard's trusted friend. I could call the Wizard, but he'll be sleeping. He won't like being bothered. And if I argue, Lord Blade may call the Wizard himself, and then I will be in trouble. What the devil! Two Wolves will keep him out of mischief, if he's got any in mind. The Wolf turned to pull the bell cord.

The two Wolves came out within a couple of minutes. They threw Serana a sour look, but that meant nothing.

The Wolves openly despised the house guards as soft, half-trained, and untrustworthy. The house guards considered the Wolves bloodthirsty maniacs. Loyalty to the Wizard and the Wolves' superiority as fighters kept the peace between them.

Now the little procession of four tramped down another succession of halls and stairways, to the wing of the castle that held the Great Hall with the view-balls and sky-bridges. The entrance had two doors, separated by a small room with benches along one wall. Here the house guards and other people not admitted to the Great Hall were allowed to wait. The outer door was guarded by Wolves. The inner door was guarded by fear of the Wizard's magic and of the punishments inflicted on those who broke important rules. They not only died, they died slowly, at the hands of the Wizard's executioners, the Wolves, and sometimes even the Wizard himself—or so the tales ran.

Serana settled herself on the bench, doing her best to seem perfectly calm under the eyes of four Wolves. Blade wished he didn't have to leave her out there, with a job to do that would need a cool head, good timing, and some strength. The cool head and the timing she had, but Blade wondered about the strength.

Unfortunately, they had no choice, because there was no way to get a Wolf outfit for Serana. Disguised as a house guard, she had to wait outside the Great Hall. Doing anything else would give the alarm at once. If the alarm went up before the assistant on duty activated the sky-gate to Kassaro,

Blade and Serana could hope for nothing better than a quick death. Here in the Great Hall, so close to the Wolf barracks, they wouldn't even be able to get out and strike down the Wizard before they died. It would be a bloody and futile ending.

One of the Wolves opened the inner door and the other led Blade through. The door shut behind them, and they were in the Great Hall. It stretched two hundred feet from the door to the huge stained-glass window at the far end, lit by flickering lanterns on iron brackets and thick candles in chandeliers. On one side ran the shelves holding the crystals for the sky-bridges in their chests, on the other side the shelves holding the view-balls. A carved plaque under each ball or chest showed where it was tuned to reach.

Between the shelves were curtained alcoves with shelves for books and scrolls. These were the private studies of the Wizard's assistants. One of them was sitting at his desk as Blade entered. He saw Blade, rose, and came toward him.

"What is your pleasure, Lord Blade?" the assistant asked, bowing politely. The Wizard's assistants wore medieval-style academic gowns with hoods. This one had his hood thrown back, revealing an apple-cheeked face under close-cropped brown hair. Blade recognized the assistant as one of the youngest, pleasant and unfailingly polite. It was almost a pity that the young man had to die. On the other hand, his death at Blade's hands would be cleaner than the one awaiting him from his master, if Blade escaped.

"I wish to go to Kassaro with these two Wolves," said Blade.

"Kassaro? Yes, my lord. Do you wish me to activate its view-ball and see what the weather may be?"

Blade shook his head. "We won't be out in it that long. You can spare yourself the trouble."

"Yes, my lord." The assistant turned away and went to the shelf where an iron chest sat above a plaque reading KAS-SARO. He took the chest down, set it on the floor, pulled two steel locking pins, and opened the lid. The two fist-size square-cut crystals lying on their bed of red velvet seemed to double the light in the hall.

It was just his imagination, Blade told himself. The crystals didn't really glow, not until they'd become active. Yet it was still hard for him to be completely calm and clearheaded in the presence of the crystals. What they represented was simply too awesome to grasp easily, even though he'd been trying now for months. It was a feeling Blade didn't have very often, and didn't like when he had it. He still remained powerless to resist it when he saw the crystals.

The assistant was now placing the crystals in the center of the hall, on a green rug with a pattern of silver rays. If Blade and the Wolves had been riding out on heudas, the assistant would have taken the crystals down to a large room near the stables. As it was, they could simply walk across the sky-bridge from the hall.

As the assistant began the slow, regular breathing that would put him into the activation trance, Blade estimated distances and times. The two Wolves were standing close together, between Blade and the door. Both wore backplates and breastplates and helmets and carried slung crossbows. One had a sword, the other had an oversized mace, and both carried daggers.

It wasn't going to be easy to put them out of action fast enough, but it wouldn't be impossible. As long as the assistant didn't have time to deactivate the crystals and break the sky-bridge—

The young man began the slow chanting of the arcane syllables that accompanied the mental effort involved in activating the crystals. A hand rested lightly on each one.

Slowly the crystals began to glow, then to vibrate slightly. A faint humming began, rapidly growing louder.

The Wolves' attention was now totally on the crystals and the man sitting behind them. Even the Wizard's Wolves never quite got used to seeing the Wizard's "magic" at work. It was a pity they couldn't be struck down now, when they'd be completely off their guard. Blade knew he had to wait, until the assistant rose to his feet, clear of his trance, and pronounced the sky-bridge opened. Then it would be good for at least half an hour. Nothing that happened to the assistant could affect it, unless he had the chance to deactivate it. He wouldn't need much of a chance, either. A single minute would be enough. Blade had to have both Wolves down within that minute, or—

Suddenly the crystals flared up to twice their former brightness and vibrated so fiercely they seemed to blur. Then the glow steadied and the vibration faded away. The Great Hall was silent for a moment. Then the assistant shook his head and rose to his feet.

111

"Lord Blade, the way to Kassaro is open."

"Thank you," said Blade. As the words left his lips, both hands shot out, gripping the assistant by the collar and one sleeve of his robe. Before anyone could react, Blade spun the young man around, rammed a knee into his back, then flung him violently at the two Wolves. He sprawled almost at their feet, and they sprang apart. Blade followed the assistant and was on the first Wolf before the man could draw a weapon.

Blade's first slash glanced off the man's helmet and tore his sleeve. The second drew blood from his left arm. Before Blade could strike again the Wolf raised his mace and swung savagely. Mace and sword met with a clang and a spray of sparks. The sword flew out of Blade's hand, but he moved smoothly into another attack, gripping the man's weapon arm by wrist and elbow, then heaving violently. The Wolf screamed as his elbow shattered, then screamed again as Blade brought a knee up into his groin.

The Wolf's screams echoed up and down the Great Hall. As if in reply, there was a burst of shouting at the entrance, cut off instantly by a squealing crash as the outer door slid shut. Serana had done her job. The Great Hall was sealed off.

The other Wolf realized what the closed door meant as quickly as Blade. He charged off down the hall like a sprinter, waving his sword and shouting. Blade saw the first Wolf was out of the fight, but the assistant was crawling on hands and knees toward the crystals. Blade's sword came down, and the assistant's body jerked like a gaffed fish as his head rolled away across the carpet. Then Blade dashed after the second Wolf.

The man was through the inner door before Blade caught him. Swords clanged fiercely in the entrance chamber, and Blade heard Serana scream. He heaved the inner door open, to see the Wolf backing Serana into a corner a step at a time. Her rough and ready swordsmanship wouldn't keep her alive much longer, not against a trained Wolf. Fortunately it wouldn't have to.

The Wolf heard rather than saw Blade come into the room behind him and knew what had to be done. His sword whistled in a deadly arc toward Serana's head, smashing down her guard. Blade had the sick knowledge that Serana was going to be dead in the next moment, even if the Wolf was dead the moment after that.

Then Serana dropped to the floor, taking the Wolf's sword

112

across her helmet. The helmet flew off, but the sword glanced off to strike the wall. Before the Wolf could swing again, Blade came up behind him and gripped the man by the throat in both hands. Serana bounced to her feet, her dagger drawn. As Blade jerked back, snapping the Wolf's neck, Serana thrust the dagger into the man's left eye, plunging it through to the brain. The Wolf writhed convulsively for a moment, blood gushing from his nose and mouth, then went limp.

Blade threw the second bolt on the door, clamped the two iron padlocks into place, and dropped the iron-strapped wooden bar into its brackets. Fists and swords hammered wildly on the door from outside, but Blade ignored them. It would now take a full-sized battering ram to break down the outer door. All the Wolves in Rentoro couldn't hurt him and Serana, as long as they were on the wrong side of the door.

Only after fastening the door could Blade spare attention for Serana. She was leaning against one wall, shaking her head and rubbing her neck.

"Are you hurt?"

She slowly shook her head. "No. Just a little dizzy."

"Good. Come on." He grabbed her by the hand and led her back into the Great Hall. The first Wolf was on his feet, stumbling wide-eyed toward the door, both arms hanging useless. There seemed to be no fight in him. Serana let out a wordless growl. She rushed at the Wolf, her sword held out in front of her like a lance, drove the point into his throat, and stepped back as he tottered. He didn't fall quickly enough for her, so she stabbed him again, this time in the groin. Now he went down, and as he lay twitching on the floor Serana brought the sword down across his exposed neck. The head rolled free, helmet and all, and the Wolf lay still. Serana wiped her sword on the dead man's clothes and sheathed it with an air of satisfaction.

"He was the worst of those who had me, the night the Wizard gave me to the Wolves," she said calmly. "I thank fate I was able to face him before leaving this place and leave him dead at my feet."

Blade said nothing, for there was nothing to say. Instead he turned to the shelves holding the sky-bridge crystals. Quickly he found the chest for Morina, opened it, took out the crystals, wrapped them in the velvet, and dropped the entire package in his belt pouch. He might not be able to take the

113

Wizard back to Home Dimension with him, but he could certainly take samples of the crystal.

The hammering and shouting outside were growing louder. Serana was pulling on the dead assistant's robe over her guard's clothing. Blade walked over to the shelves holding the view-balls. The one for Morina was on the top shelf, a good eight feet above the floor. A ladder leaned against the wall at one end of the shelves. Blade shifted it, climbed up, took the heavy view-ball off its stand, and held it high over his head. Then he threw it down on the bare floor as hard as he could.

There was a crash like a thousand windows all shattering together, and yellow vapor boiled up. Blade caught a whiff of it, coughed, and wondered for a moment if he'd released a poisonous gas into the hall. Then the vapor sank down and vanished, leaving a broad yellow stain on the floor all around the fragments of the ball.

"Now the Wizard cannot see into Morina, until he makes and tunes a new view-ball," said Blade. "Before he can do that, we may give him more important things to think about."

Serana said nothing, but the look in her eyes said a great deal. Blade climbed down the ladder, wishing he had time to smash every view-ball on the shelves. That would really cripple the Wizard, but it would also take more time than was safe. Urged on by their desperate master, the Wolves might come up with some surprises, and there were always the Wizard's mental attacks to fear.

Now for the sky-bridge. Blade took Serana's hand and they walked toward the glowing crystals. She hesitated for a moment, but he urged her forward. Three steps to go, two, one—

—a sudden roaring in their ears, with the floor seeming to heave upward under them and then fall back—

—and they were standing on a brush-grown rocky hillside, in the lee of a clump of small trees. Behind them glowed the two outer crystals of the sky-bridge. Serana started down the hill, but Blade caught her arm.

"Wait. I have to smash these crystals, so no one will be able to follow us across the bridge." He gripped the mace in both hands, raised it high overhead, and brought it down with all his strength.

An inert sky-bridge crystal had to be struck exactly right to break. An activated one would shatter at a tap. The mace came down, golden light flared, and the crystal dissolved into faintly glowing powder. Blade raised the mace again, and brought it down on the second crystal, which had begun to glow more brightly.

For a second he felt as if he'd been dropped into a blast furnace. Searing light and heat were all around him, and a roaring like massed artillery fire filled his ears. He dropped the mace, jumped back, fell, and rolled several yards down the slope. He ended up almost on top of Serana, nestled against two boulders.

The glare faded and the roar died away. Blade rose and climbed back up the slope. Where the second crystal had been was now a foot-wide pit of smoking green glass. Around it the earth was blackened for several yards in all directions. The mace lay at the edge of the blackened earth, reduced to a six-inch stump of charcoal.

Blade realized now that all his exposed skin felt like a bad case of sunburn. His eyebrows and eyelashes also seemed to be missing. He was going to look rather odd for a few days. But then he'd been practically on top of the explosion of a fair-sized bomb. He'd really been quite lucky.

He returned to Serana and helped her to her feet. "It's time we went on our way," he said. "Which way is Kassaro?"

She looked around briefly to get her bearings, then pointed off into the darkness at the foot of the hill. Hand in hand they started down the slope.

Chapter 18

Blade and Serana went to a livery stable at the east end of Kassaro and hired two heudas. They were a strange sight—Blade with his scorched face and bloodstained clothing, Serana with the badly fitting assistant's robe belted on over men's clothing. The stablekeeper looked hard at them, but he looked even harder at the gold coins Blade held out to him. Silently he led them to the stables and gave them what they wanted.

It was a moonless night, black as a coal mine and with a rising wind. Blade and Serana left Kassaro and trotted across the wooden bridge, then spurred their heudas to a gallop.

The darkness not only hid them from prying eyes, it nearly hid the road from them. Fortunately it was straight and paved all the way to Morina. Otherwise they would probably have ridden into one of the streams the road crossed on its way to the city.

They were halfway to Morina when a cold rain began whipping into their faces. The rain grew steadily heavier, until they had to slow to a trot, then to a walk. Serana gave an animal snarl of frustration at the loss of time, but Blade reassured her.

"We've nothing to fear. In this rain we could pass five yards from a thousand Wolves without their seeing us."

By the time the walls of Morina loomed out of the storm, both Blade and Serana were as wet as if they really had ridden into a stream. Serana rose in her stirrups and hailed the sentries on the gate. She had to shout three times before she could make herself heard over the roar of the wind and the rain.

"Who be, and what business?" at last came down from above.

"Two of Morina, returning on lawful affairs. We are

116

bound for Haymi's Fountain and bear a message from Grasso."

Morina closed its gates at nightfall and opened them at dawn. During the hours of darkness, people could be admitted only if they gave a specific destination and had someone there prepared to assume responsibility for them. Haymi's Fountain was a well-known tavern and lodging house, one of the meeting places for the Wizard's enemies in Morina. "A message from Grasso" was code, meaning that a person came on business of great importance to the rebels. When that message reached the Fountain, someone there would be willing to assume responsibility for Blade and Serana.

"At least it was the right message, two years ago," whispered Serana. "They have doubtless changed the code, but we can hope someone will remember the old one. Otherwise we shall not be getting into Morina tonight."

They waited, sitting on their heudas as the rain poured down. They could not get any colder or wetter, and in the darkness no one was likely to recognize Serana. Blade still would not be at ease until they were safely inside Haymi's Fountain. If the gate guards did make them wait out here all night, they'd have to enter the city in daylight, when the crowd would certainly include some men in the pay of the Wizard.

At last Blade heard the groan and squeal of ponderous hinges moving, and one of the gates swung open. They rode through the gateway into a narrow street, with tall houses crowding close on either side. Three men with swords and bows but no armor came down from the gatehouse. One walked ahead, two behind, and the little party tramped through the rain-soaked streets to Haymi's Fountain.

Serana did not speak until they were safely inside a dank cellar room far below the level of the street. The walls were lined with immense wine barrels, trailing tufts of cobweb. Behind the barrels Blade could hear the scurrying of rats.

At last the shuffle of many feet sounded outside the heavy door. Only one man came in through the doorway, but Blade knew there must be at least half a dozen waiting outside. He and Serana had been trusted this far, because of the "message from Grasso." They weren't going any farther until they'd explained themselves, and they might not even leave this room alive if they couldn't explain.

Haymi Razence looked as if some of the rats in his cellars

were his relatives. He was barely five feet tall with a narrow face that seemed all nose and eyes. Lank black hair, thinning on top, trailed down on either side of his skull. In his belt he wore an unsheathed dagger nearly as long as his arm.

"Grasso has sent you?" Razence said. His voice was surprisingly deep for a man his size.

"Yes," said Blade, and Serana nodded.

"You know that Grasso has given way in favor of Teodarn?"

"I did not," said Blade.

"I think you had better tell me why you did not know this," said Haymi. He backed away until he was just outside Blade's striking range, and his hand fell to his dagger hilt.

Serana slammed both hands down on the table, startling Razence into drawing his dagger. He was opening his mouth to call in the men outside when Serana stood up, stepped out from behind the table, and pulled the hood of her robe back from her face. Her hair had grown several inches since Blade began visiting her. Now she pulled it back, took a ribbon from her pouch, and tied her hair in a ragged pile on top of her head.

Razence's mouth opened wider and wider, but no sound came out. His fingers went limp and the dagger clattered to the floor.

Blade was tempted to pick it up, but instead said quietly, "Yes. It is the Lady Serana Zotair, back from the castle of the Wizard. She is not a ghost, and neither am I. Together we have escaped from the castle, and we bear with us all the Wizard's secrets."

"You are—" Razence finally got his mouth closed long enough to get out a couple of words.

"I am Richard Blade, a traveler, warrior, and learned man. I am also an enemy of the Wizard, and wish to see Rentoro free of his power. I believe this can be done."

Razence was now looking from Blade to Serana to the door and back to Blade. He was obviously wondering who in this room was mad—the man, the woman, himself, or all of them? Then Serana laughed.

"Haymi Razence, you doubt that I am Serana? Do not doubt it. I am the same Serana who helped your brother Murga bury the hunting dog Silver, just east of the three willows at the north bend of the River Oti, opposite the manor of Lord Figua."

At this point Haymi Razence gave a remarkably good imitation of a man about to fall down in a fit. Blade started forward to help him, then stopped as Serana burst out laughing.

"Poor Haymi," she said, when she caught her breath. "He will get over his shock soon enough. What I told him proves that I am indeed Serana. Murga Razence was one of my few playmates when I was a girl. Once we took out a hunting dog of my father's without his permission, and the poor beast was bitten by a snake. So we buried him secretly and said he ran off. Haymi is the only one we told the truth. No one could know exactly where we buried Silver except Murga and I, and Murga is dead." The laughter died out of her face and voice. "He was poisoned by the Wizard's spies." Then she sat down again, waiting with a queen's dignity for Haymi to get his voice back and put his thoughts in order. Her impatience showed in a foot that tapped steadily and a hand that clenched and unclenched itself.

She seemed very much in command and that was her right. This was her city, these were her people, and the dream of being free of the Wizard really belonged to the Rentorans. Blade had given them the key to victory, but from now on the fight was bound to be mostly in their hands.

Eventually Razence regained both his wits and his voice, sent his guards away, and drew up a chair. "Now, my lady, and Lord Blade—what secrets of the Wizard's magic do you bring from his castle?"

"All of them," said Blade simply, and Serana nodded.

"If we act swiftly on what Blade has learned," she said, "Morina can be free of the Wizard's power within weeks. All of Rentoro can be free before the snow falls. The Wizard may survive for a time, shut up in his castle. But it will have become his prison, not the seat of his power."

"The Lady Serana speaks the truth," said Blade. He fixed the innkeeper with a level stare. "She has also spoken to me of how some of those who hate the Wizard are slow to act. Or at least they were two years ago, when she was taken to the Wizard's castle. What will the Wizard's enemies in Morina be ready to do now?"

Razence took a deep breath. "If you can tell us how to break the power of the Wizard's magic, we will listen. We will do more than listen—we will strike. As long as we have some hope of victory, you may command us and we will obey."

"It will still be dangerous," said Serana quietly.

Razence's thin shoulders straightened. "That is doubtless true. But we are prepared to die under the swords of the Wolves, as long as we know that our children will not." He turned to Blade. "Do not think that the men of Morina have ever been cowards, Lord Blade. It is easy enough to be brave when you risk no life but your own. It is less easy, when you know that you will see your father gelded, your wife ravished, your children flung from walls or spitted on swords, and then be burned yourself by slow fire."

"I understand," said Blade. "But that is at an end. First of all, the Wizard is not truly a magician. All his knowledge and arts are of this world, although many are not within the grasp of ordinary men. He is a very wise man, who has turned all his wisdom to evil."

Blade went on from there, explaining everything he could about the Wizard without mentioning the man's origins. He didn't need to. The strategy they'd be using against the Wizard would be the same whether he'd come from Renaissance Italy or fallen from the sky as the legends said.

Razence managed to keep up with Blade's explanations, although he was obviously having to make an enormous mental effort to do so. Several times he asked Blade to repeat something and twice he asked Blade to stop entirely. Finally he rose, shaking his head like a man waking from a particularly vivid dream.

"I cannot decide on this matter by myself. Our people now have seven leaders, and I am only one of them."

"Seven?" Serana frowned. "Isn't that letting too many know too much?"

Razence shrugged. "It might be, except that we cannot keep that much secret for long, no matter how hard we try. So we contrive as best we can. Even the Wizard's magic—"

"The Wizard's mental powers, Haymi," said Serana gently.

"The Wizard's powers, then," said the little man. "Even they cannot watch seven men all at once. Nor can his assassins slay seven men in a single night."

"I understand," said Blade. "Very well. Have the other six come here tomorrow, and I will tell them what I've told you. Then we can—"

"But the danger!" exploded Razence. "The Wizard's magic eye can fall on us, and he will then know—!"

120

Blade and Serana broke into roars of laughter. After a moment Razence blushed and sheepishly joined the laughter. Finally he shook his head. "I am sorry, my lady, my lord. My wits have never been the fastest in Morina, and what you have told me has not made them any faster. I forgot that the Wizard can no longer see anything in Morina, except through the eyes of his hired dogs." His face became a grim mask that made Blade very glad he was not one of the Wizard's spies. "But how shall I protect them when they come?"

"The same way you were going to protect yourself against us," said Blade. "Call your guards and post them at the doors to the Fountain. Let no one in or out until the men have gone."

"Yes, yes, I can do that," said Razence. He seemed to be eager to show that he understood Blade, whether he really did or not.

"Also do not send anyone out to kill the Wizard's spies until you can kill them all at once," said Blade gently. "Otherwise some will get away."

"Yes, yes, that also is true," said Razence. With a visible effort he straightened up. "Now, is there?"

"Yes," said Serana. "You can give us one of your private rooms."

"One room?"

"Yes."

"Together?"

"Yes." Serana's voice now had a bite to it. "Haymi, you ask too many questions. Go have the room prepared, and also a hot bath and as much food as you can find. We've come a long way, we're soaked to the skin, and we're hungry enough to roast you in your own hearth if we don't get fed and quickly!"

"Certainly, my lady. It shall all be done. At once." Haymi backed away, nearly tripped over his own heels, and vanished out the door.

Blade shook his head. It looked as if he might have to go on giving orders in Morina after all. At least he'd have to until the people here realized what was happening and started thinking for themselves. He hoped the other six leaders of the rebels wouldn't be thrown into such confusion, but he wasn't going to hope for too much. He pulled up a chair beside Serana and sat with his arm around her until a boy came down to tell them their baths were ready.

121

Bathed and with a meal of beef, bread, and wine inside him, Blade began to feel more like a human being. He sat on the great chest at the foot of the bed in their room and raised his cup.

"To a free Rentoro."

Serana smiled and reached over to clink her cup against his, then drank. "Now, Blade," she said, "you are coming to bed." It was a command, not a question or even a polite request.

Blade stood up. "I thought you'd be fit for nothing but sleep, after this night."

"Perhaps I once thought so too, but now I find that I don't. Blade, do you remember how much we hoped to some day share a bed without having to deceive the Wizard? Do you think I didn't hope for that as much as you?" She slid off the bed and came toward him, unknotting the sash of her chamber robe as she came. The golden flowered silk slipped to the floor and she reached him wearing nothing but perfume and her golden hair.

Then her perfumed beauty was pressing against Blade, and her lips were on his as if they wanted to suck out his life. He could feel her trembling with desire, feel his own desire rising to match hers, as she led him toward the bed.

Chapter 19

Blade explained the Wizard's secrets and his own campaign plan three times the next day.

The first time he explained it to Haymi Razence and the other six leaders of the rebels against the Wizard in Morina. The second time he explained it to the four leaders of the rebels' strong-arm guards and assassins, who would be sent against the Wizard's spies and agents in the city.

Both times he had to go slowly, since he faced men who could hardly believe what they were hearing. Both times he was interrupted at almost every other sentence by a cry of surprise or some confused question. Both times he gradually saw belief awakening on drawn faces, then hope, then joy. He listened to wild cheering and was pounded on the back until he was sure he'd be black and blue. One of the assassins, a man as tough-looking as any Wolf leader, broke down and sobbed like a child.

Blade wasn't surprised. The Wizard had a peculiar method for dealing with opponents in the larger cities. He did not try to kill them off the moment they appeared. Instead he used the view-balls and his spies to keep watch on them. When they seemed about to become dangerous, he sent in the Wolves. Sometimes he struck only at the guilty men, sometimes at their families or friends as well. Sometimes he would even take a man's wife or child and leave the man himself.

Even when a group of rebels showed no signs of becoming dangerous, the Wizard would sooner or later strike it down. There was no way of predicting when this would happen. It seemed to be guided entirely by the Wizard's whims. In Morina the Wizard struck more often, because of the city's history. The Wizard's enemies there had been virtually destroyed five times in the last forty years.

So every leader Blade spoke to was a man under a sort of suspended death sentence—a sentence the Wizard might impose at any time. None of them could go to bed at night certain they would live to see another dawn. Now Blade had offered them hope.

The third time Blade explained the Wizard's secrets and the campaign against him, he had an audience of only one man. That man, however, was Count Drago Bossir, and he was worth ten ordinary Morinans.

"We must win him over, Blade," said Serana. "If my brother himself were to come over to our cause, he could hardly do more for it."

"I will do my best," replied Blade. "But it seems to me that Count Drago must be half converted already, or he would not have taken the risk of coming here."

"Do not for one moment let him know you think that," said Serana urgently. "Then he will be as stubborn as an old mule, just out of pride."

It seemed to Blade that the count had good reason to be both proud and stubborn—if only because he was still alive at eighty. He'd survived more of the history of the Wizard's rule than anyone else alive in Morina.

He'd been only two when Morina rose in its last great rebellion against the Wizard and the last great battle against the Wolves was fought outside its walls. His father and one uncle died in the battle, another uncle was burned alive, and his mother was carried off to be a plaything for the Wolves. He himself survived only by the Wolves' carelessness.

He survived, and over the next seventy years suffered from the Wizard's tyranny time after time. He was betrothed to a young woman, and the Wolves took her for the Wizard's harem. He married, had three children, and lost two of them to the Wizard. A son went to the crystal mines, while a daughter was caught up in a plot against the Wizard and died slowly and painfully from an assassin's poison. Of his grandchildren, Zemun now commanded a company in the city guard. The other, Nebon, was a fugitive since five years ago and very probably long dead.

In spite of his years and his sufferings, the count looked no more than sixty. He held himself as straight as a lance, and there was still more gray than white in his pointed beard and flowing hair. His voice was low, but not from weakness. It was the quiet voice of a man who knows he has only a certain amount of strength left, and will not waste a bit of it.

Count Drago listened calmly as Blade explained the

124

Wizard and the coming war against him. When he'd finished, the count's head sank down on his chest and there was a long silence. Blade wondered if the old man was falling asleep, then noticed that the gray eyes under the bushy brows were bright and wet. He was silent, until suddenly the count's head snapped up and those eyes fixed themselves on Blade.

"I will be with you, on one condition," he said.

Blade and Serana spoke almost together. "What is that?"

"The Bossirs are a family as old as the Zotairs. Perhaps the Lady Serana did not tell you this, Blade, but it is true." Serana nodded reluctantly. "We are also as worthy to rule Morina. More worthy, considering how Duke Efrim has played pimp to the Wizard these past five years." Serana frowned, but nodded again.

"I have endured much, for longer than either of you has been alive," the count went on. "All my dead, you know of them. All the shame, perhaps you do not know. I am alive myself, only because I have pretended all those dead were nothing to me. No one has heard me speak a word against the Wizard, until now. I have lived for the last sixty years by imitating a rabbit."

Blade found it hard to imagine a less appropriate comparison. The count reminded him far more of an old wolf, grown gray but far from toothless. If this old wolf did bite, the Wizard and the Wizard's friends were going to feel his teeth.

"You have lived sixty years as a rabbit," said Serana briskly. "Now you wish to end your life as a man. How can we help you?"

"As I said, the Bossirs are fit to rule Morina. I would be Duke of Morina, and my grandson and his heirs after me."

Serana sprang out of her chair, her face turning red with sudden rage. Blade gripped her by both shoulders until the rage passed. She still seemed unable to find words, so Blade spoke.

"You ask much, Count Drago."

"I deserve much, after so many years."

"Does the Lady Serana deserve to be cast aside, after all that she has endured in the Wizard's castle?"

"She will not be cast aside. I imagine my grandson Zemun will be more than happy to marry her. She will have a place worthy of her, never fear. Or do you have hopes of marrying her yourself?"

Blade smiled. "She will be an excellent wife for any man who weds her, but that man will not be me. When the Wizard's power is broken, I must continue on my travels."

The count seemed to relax. Obviously he'd been afraid that Blade was another adventurer like the Wizard, a man who might not wish to rule all of Rentoro, but who could have ambitions in Morina. "My grandson would agree with you about the merits of the Lady Serana. Shall we—"

"Shall you two stop discussing me as though I was a prize mare?" Serana snapped. "I think I have some right to speak, when my fate and that of my house is being decided."

"Certainly," said the count. "But we thought you had nothing to say." His face and voice became grave. "My lady, the House of Zotair has come to the end of its road, or it will have soon—"

"My brother lives. He is young, his wife is fertile, and he has a son."

"Two sons, Serana. There is a second, born a year ago."

"So why do you reach out your hand for the duchy, then?" Serana's rage seemed to be past, but there was still an edge in her voice. Blade didn't blame her. The ambitions of Count Drago's old age threatened at least to weaken Morina in its fight against the Wizard. At least? That was more than enough!

"Because none of this will make the slightest difference, when open warfare begins against the Wizard," said the count sharply. "Your brother will do something that will raise every hand in Morina against him."

"He hasn't yet."

"He will. He lives today only because people fear his master, the Wizard. You have been away from Morina these past two years, Serana. You could not hope to know how your brother has gone from bad to worse in kissing the Wizard's ass and indulging his own vices. The House of Zotair is doomed, except for you. Your brother's wife will die with him, and the sons are too young to rule for many years. We cannot afford a child-duke and a regency for so long, not after the fall of the Wizard."

Blade smiled. "You seem very confident that we are going to fight the Wizard and win. Then why do you think we need your help so badly that Serana must give up her family's position in your favor?"

"I just said it. That position isn't going to be worth a pile

126

of sheep dung!" snapped the count. His patience was clearly beginning to wear as thin as Serana's. "Do not think that I will lift a finger against you if you challenge the Wizard. I will be happy to see his power broken, whatever else may or may not happen. But I will be happier to see Morina in the hands of my house. My voice speaking for you is perhaps worth that much."

Blade knew the count's proposal had to be seriously considered, whether Serana liked it or not. From what Blade had heard, the count was one of the most respected men in Morina. His call could bring out many people who might otherwise waver, at least during the next few weeks. Those weeks would be the crucial ones in preparing Morina for the war, and even a few extra men at work might make a great difference when the Wolves came down.

They might gain even more than time and willing hands. With the count on their side, Duke Efrim would find it harder to wage open warfare against them. He simply would not be able to find enough fighting men. Blade and Serana would still have to worry about the Wolves, the Wizard's assassins, and probably the duke's treachery. They would not have to fight and win a civil war in Morina before they could face the Wolves.

Certainly that was worth something. If the count was right, the Zotairs were finished anyway. All he wanted in return for his help was the assurance of an orderly succession for the Bossirs. That would certainly be a blessing to Morina as well as to the Bossirs. Otherwise there might not be a civil war before they met the Wolves, but there would almost certainly be one afterward.

Destroying the Wizard's power was going to reintroduce traditional politics to Rentoro, Blade realized. Every rivalry and feud simmering over the last century was going to boil over at once. The battle that destroyed the Wolves was going to be only the first in a long and probably bloody series.

Well, Rentoro was still going to be better off without the Wizard's tyranny. But it might take some time. Meanwhile, there was the question of Count Drago's proposal, facing them here and now.

Blade looked at Serana and she nodded at him to go ahead. "Count Drago," he said. "We cannot throw away the House of Zotair merely on your word. The Lady Serana has been away for two years, and I have never been in Morina until now. We do not know all that we need to know. Let us ask certain other men about these matters. If they speak as you have done, we can meet here in—oh, two days. Then you will find us more ready to talk of your proposal."

Blade was afraid the count would explode at the implication he was not telling the truth. However, he merely blinked, then nodded slowly. "Your bargaining would shame a heuda-dealer," he said with a thin smile. "But I would not have it otherwise, if you are going to be a leader in this war against the Wizard. Very well, in two days' time." He rose and left without another word.

Serana let out a sigh that made the candles flicker. "That old—! People always said there was more to him than met the eye, but I never dreamed of this! I don't much love Efrim, but by all the fates I hope Drago's lying about him!"

"And if he isn't?" said Blade quietly. He wanted to thrash the matter out with Serana now, in case they didn't see eye to eye. They would be wise to present a united front the next time they faced the count.

Serana sighed again. "If he isn't, then he can have Morina, and much good may it do him! Yet—can there be so many people who might oppose us, that we need the count's support? Can anyone in Morina dream of supporting the Wizard, when they know they must fight him or die?"

"Yes," said Blade wearily. "There will always be those who don't believe that's the choice. Even among those who do believe, many will hope to save their own skins by going on their knees to the Wizard. We could shout ourselves blue in the face and none of them would change. They may listen to the count."

"It seems the fates have filled Morina with fools," Serana growled.

"It is no worse than other cities," said Blade. "And now, all this talk has made me thirsty." He picked up the handbell and rang for a servant.

Chapter 20

During the next two days Blade and Serana sent out more than polite questions about the popularity of Duke Efrim and the House of Zotair. They refused to wait on Count Drago's ambitions.

They sent out messages to every important man in Morina, telling them that the city was doomed unless it rose against the Wizard. If Morina did rise, on the other hand, it might lead all of Rentoro in a mighty war to end the Wizard's rule.

They sent other messages to every craftsman in Morina or within a day's ride of the city. They were to start making helmets, pikes, bows and arrows, and battleaxes, as fast as possible and as many as possible. When the Wolves came, the Morinans would probably be unarmored, but hopefully not unarmed.

They sent still more messages to Count Drago's grandson Zemun and the other officers of the city guards. They were to keep the gates absolutely closed all night. During the day, they were to search every man, woman, heuda, and wagon going in or out. Anyone caught with certain items was to be arrested and turned over to Blade and Serana.

Serana sent a short letter to her brother:

Brother Efrim,
  By now you have doubtless learned that I am in Morina, and what I mean to do. I wish to remain at peace with you, if you permit it. But I shall not permit anyone to stand in the way of what I shall do for Morina. The decision is yours.

Your sister Serana

Serana sent an armed escort with the messenger who carried this letter to the ducal palace.

"Just in case my brother loses his temper so that the messenger's in danger of losing his head," she said, with a grin. "Efrim's a hot-tempered man at times."

"That letter won't cool him down," said Blade.

"No. But I've always wanted a chance to write to him like that. Now I've got it."

Finally Blade and Serana sent out the rebels' assassins against the Wizard's spies. The faster these men were dead or out of circulation, the better for Morina.

The Wizard's spies had received a message that there was a crisis at hand, but not that they themselves were in danger. The Wizard's lapse was fatal for his spies in Morina. Twenty of them were killed within a few hours, another dozen rounded up and questioned roughly but effectively before being killed. They revealed the names of many more spies, who were in turn rounded up and questioned.

By the time the dust settled, the Wizard had lost more than fifty men. Their severed heads were piled into a large basket and the basket hung from a fountain in the main square of Morina. To the basket a sign was pinned:

THESE MEN SERVED THE WIZARD. ALL WHO SERVE HIM WILL MEET THE SAME FATE.

Serana Zotair

"No doubt there are a good many more spies whose names we haven't learned," said Serana. "But they may be less enthusiastic after seeing what happened to their comrades."

"There's also the effect on your brother," Blade said. "He may realize that daggers can strike down dukes as well as spies. That might frighten him into keeping quiet."

"It may also frighten him into striking out like a madman," Serana said grimly. "We shall see."

If Duke Efrim did strike out, he was going to find it hard to do anything against Blade and Serana. They were no longer keeping their headquarters at Haymi's Fountain. Instead they were in a large room on the second floor of the town house of a merchant who was one of the rebel leaders. More than fifty armed men guarded the house and watched the streets around it. Blade and Serana wore chain mail under their clothes during the day and ate and drank nothing that hadn't been tasted for them. No handful of the Wizard's assassins would get through to them. It would take a small army and that meant Duke Efrim.

By sending that army the duke would be declaring war against his own people, as an ally of the Wizard. Then whatever happened to Morina, he would not live to see it. Blade, Serana, and the rebellion's leaders knew this. If Duke Efrim knew it as well, it might keep the peace in Morina.

One by one the messengers sent to ask about the future of the House of Zotair returned. One by one they reported. As they reported, Serana's face became steadily grimmer. She'd suspected Count Drago might be telling the truth, but it still hurt to have him confirmed by half the noblemen and great merchants of Morina.

"The House of Zotair *has* come to the end of its road," she said with a weary sigh. "My brother could come out into the public streets and denounce the Wizard at the top of his lungs. He'd still be torn to bits before he could finish speaking. Never mind for the moment all he's done for the Wizard. He and his drinking companions have broken too many heads, raped too many women, burned or smashed too many shops. Even when they're only amusing themselves they behave like Wolves in a rebellious town.

"I myself am not hated. I am honored for what I have endured at the Wizard's hands, respected, even loved. No one in Morina wishes me harm, but no one wishes to see me in power if it means the Zotairs will still be ruling."

"What about Efrim's sons?" asked Blade.

"What about them?" replied Serana with a shrug. "They are a little boy and a baby. A regency is the last thing Morina needs after all that will happen before the Wizard falls."

Blade nodded, relieved. He'd only raised the point to make sure Serana herself was convinced that a regency was too dangerous. It was obvious such an arrangement could not provide Morina with the strong leadership it needed. Blade also suspected it could not stand against Serana's ambitions, if she chose to make trouble. She might be willing to put those ambitions aside for the time being; he found it hard to believe she could put them aside forever.

"I think it's time we sent for Count Drago," Blade said.

Count Drago came, wearing an ancient coat of mail dug out of some secret closet. His face was pale and drawn, as if he'd been sleeping less than usual the past two nights.

131

"You look like a ghost," said Serana. "Sit down and have some wine and cake. You want to live to see Morina free, don't you?"

Count Drago smiled, but there was no amusement in his voice as he replied. "I am a ghost, in a way. Or at least I feel there are ghosts with me and in me." He sipped at his wine.

"Last night I dreamed of a procession of the dead, Morina's dead in a hundred years of warfare against the Wizard. My father led the procession, with his shield upon his shoulder and his skull gaping open as it did when they found his body. He spoke to me, though I do not remember what he said. Then he gave me his shield, and after that I awoke."

In spite of this voice from the past, the count was as ruthless and unsentimental as ever when it came to deciding the future of Morina. The bargaining went on all day and only came to an end over a late supper. In the end they worked out the following agreement:

(1) The Bossirs should be declared the true and proper heirs to the ducal throne by the Assembly of Morina as soon as it could lawfully meet.

(2) Count Drago would renounce any claim to the throne for himself.

(3) His surviving grandson Zemun would be proclaimed Duke of Morina upon the deposition or death of Duke Efrim.

(4) If Zemun Bossir did not survive the coming battles, Zemun's own son by his dead wife would be proclaimed heir.

(5) If Zemun's son succeeded, Count Drago would be sole Regent as long as he lived. After that there would be a Council of Regency, drawn from the Assembly and other notables.

(6) Serana would marry Zemun Bossir after the war, and become Duchess of Morina. She would also be a member of the Council of Regency if one became necessary.

There were also several dozen minor clauses, dividing up the Zotair estates, awarding this or that office, etc., with repeated references to the count's will. Serana's dowery rights, and much else. By the time every point was covered, the agreement spread across several large sheets of parchment. By the time it was all drawn up with proper calligraphy and in proper legal language, it would be the size of a small book.

None of them considered the time wasted. As long as they were going to reach an agreement at all, they had to do a good job. As the count put it, "We're forging a weapon to use against the Wizard. No sensible man will ever trust a weapon that's not well made."

At last the job was done. The count was escorted home by a squad of Blade's guards and Serana led Blade to their bed. He went, but afterward asked, "Do you think we should go on sharing this room? If you are to be married to Zemun Bossir after the war—"

"Zemun Bossir will have a good and loyal wife, *after* I have married him," Serana replied. "Until our wedding day, I am by law, custom, and my own choice my own mistress. If Zemun Bossir worries about what I do now, he will only waste strength he will certainly need against the Wolves."

Then her lips began their urgent journey back and forth across Blade's body. As he lay back under their caresses, Blade thought of her last remark, and how true it was. Sooner or later, this unnatural condition that was neither war nor peace would come to a bloody end, and the Wolves would come to Morina.

Blade went up on the city's walls every morning before dawn, to watch for the smoke on the horizon and the glint of sunlight on armor that would tell him the Wolves had come. Sometimes Zemun Bossir accompanied Blade, sometimes Count Drago. Young Zemun was so happy over being heir-apparent to Morina that he was quite prepared to forgive Blade for almost anything.

"After all, Blade," he said, "I owe you far too much to feel the jealous rage of a child. I know what sort of captivity Serana endured in the Wizard's castle. I shall make her forget it all when I am duke. I shall do anything to make her forget it, anything."

"You show a good heart, Zemun. I wish you luck, and both of you much happiness."

Privately Blade sometimes thought Zemun Bossir was so enthusiastic about becoming Duke of Morina that he sometimes forgot about the coming war. Still, he seemed a good choice to rule the new Morina. He was brave, intelligent, thoroughly honest, and with a real gift for winning popularity. His company of guards would follow him through fire and water. He was also impulsive, enthusiastic, and talkative, but he'd get over that in a few more years—if he or anyone else in Morina lived that long.

The Wolves would come. It was impossible that the Wizard would let his power simply dissolve without putting up a fight to save it. So *where were the Wolves?*

Count Drago offered part of the answer. "I've read the history of every fight the Wolves have been in since I was born," he said. "I've never read of their being out for more than five or six days at a time. I've never heard of their laying siege to a city, or even using war engines in the field. Did you see any stone-throwers, wagons, tents, things like that, when you were in the castle?"

"No."

"Then the Wizard probably doesn't have any. He's like all soldiers. When they've fought one kind of war for three generations, they forget there's any other kind.

"The Wolves have been raiders, not campaigners, for three generations. They'll have to build everything they need for a long campaign, then learn how to use it, *then* march on Morina. The sky-bridges won't put them down right outside our gates this time. They'll have to ride, probably for several days, and our scouts will be watching them every foot of the way."

The count rambled on about the coming campaign against the Wolves for quite a while. Blade began to realize that one problem when the Wolves did come would be keeping Count Drago out of the fighting. His eighty years had slowed his limbs, but they hadn't dimmed his eye or his fierce hatred of the Wolves.

Blade hoped the count was right about the Wolves having to learn to become campaigners instead of raiders. If he was, Morina might have more time than Blade had dared hope. Every extra day would make it a tougher nut for the Wolves to crack.

No one in Morina was wasting any time. The weapons-makers worked as if the Wolves were already at the gates.

The forges smoked and the tools clattered morning, noon, and night. Already there were weapons for two thousand men. In another two weeks there would be enough to arm five thousand, which was nearly every man in Morina fit for war.

The men already armed were training hard, under Blade's leadership and the guidance of reliable men from Zemun Bossir's company of guards. The city's guards had been policemen and firemen as much as soldiers, but they made fairly good drillmasters. Compared to Blade, the Wizard had an easy job. He merely had to make raiders into campaigners. Blade had to make an army of men who hadn't fought or expected to fight for three generations.

Other things were being done, to make sure Morina would not be taken by surprise or have to fight alone. Mounted patrols scoured all the roads, stopping and searching travellers to make sure the Wizard's agents could not place new sky-bridge crystals close to the city. Working parties prepared ambush sites and roadblocks. Blade was taking a leaf from the Wizard's own book, setting up a defense in depth to hammer at the Wolves long before they reached the city's walls.

The most important riders were those who pounded along the roads with Blade's messages to the other cities and towns of Rentoro. Rise, he told them. Rise and be free! The Wizard has never had real magic, and now he has no secrets either. I know how we may defeat him, and free Rentoro from his grasp.

Some of the cities and towns rose against the Wizard even more enthusiastically than Morina. The Wizard's spies fled or died horribly, blacksmiths sweated forging spearpoints and helmets, and search parties scoured the countryside for sky-bridge crystals.

There were many ways to destroy the crystals, or at least make them useless. They could be thrown into a fire hot enough to melt them, crushed to powder under heavy stones, or simply picked up and carried off. Blade heard of one particularly ingenious trick used by an outlaw leader in the far north. The leader's name was Arno, and he wore a black mask to conceal a face twisted by a birth injury.

He picked up the crystals of a sky-bridge, took them to a nearby lake, and carefully dropped them into the deepest part of it. Blade wondered what would happen when the Wizard tried to activate that particular sky-bridge. Would the crystals simply not work? Would they explode, or perhaps flood the Great Hall? Even better, might the Wolves get through, to find themselves drowning thirty feet down? Blade applauded Arno's ingenuity and hoped he would be able to meet the man before he had to leave Rentoro.

Some of the scouting parties found only patrols of Wolves. Although the Wizard was not yet attacking Morina, he was not abandoning the countryside to his enemies. Small raiding parties of Wolves charged in and out of those sky-bridges that were still open. They intercepted messengers, ambushed scouts, attacked undefended farms and villages in the old style. For the moment the Wizard was using random terror against his enemies, since he had nothing else.

The Wolves did not have everything their own way. Now they faced Rentorans who'd lost most of their terror of the Wizard's magic, and knew that the Wolves were only men like themselves, no matter whom they served. The Rentorans did not fight very skilfully, and many of them died. But they fought bravely, desperately, and viciously, and a good many Wolves also died.

Meanwhile, the cities and towns were raising armies. The ones in rebellion against the Wizard were preparing to defend themselves against the Wolves. If they didn't have walls or moats, they were also digging ditches and building log palisades as fast as they could.

Other cities and towns were declaring themselves allies of the Wizard, and preparing armies to march with the Wolves against their neighbors. Serana cursed fluently when she heard this news, but admitted she wasn't greatly surprised.

"As you said, Blade, many people are going to try settling old scores or snatching someone else's land. Also, what do you wager that those cities which march with the Wizard will ask a stiff price for their aid?"

"I wouldn't wager anything," replied Blade. "I think it's a certainty. Even those people who support the Wizard won't go in awe of his magic anymore. They'll treat him as they would any other tyrant, to be supported or fought as common sense tells them. The Wizard's old power in Rentoro is already gone, and that means he's doomed, sooner or later." Blade was telling the truth, but not the whole truth. How long would it take to bring the Wizard down? It might take only a single pitched battle. It might also take ten years of savage warfare, reducing half of Rentoro to a desert. Blade kept that second possibility very much to himself.

The passing weeks turned into a month. Morina's defenders were now armed and trained. Heavy stone-throwers were being constructed, and gangs of men were cleaning out Morina's ancient moat and refilling it.

Another week. Still no Wolves, and still not a single word or action from Duke Efrim. Serana began to find her brother's silence not only mysterious, but even alarming.

"You think he's planning something?" asked Blade.

"Let's say that I can think of no other good reason for him to be silent so long," she replied. "He can control his temper if he has to. Often he lulls his enemies into believing he doesn't care, and then strikes when they're off guard."

"What would you expect him to be planning?"

"I don't know. He must know by now that he can't challenge us openly. That means treachery. How, when, where— the fates only know, and they're not telling us!"

"Perhaps we'd better pick some of our best fighters and mount them on heudas," Blade said. "That way they can reach any point inside the walls faster than men on foot. I can keep them under my personal command and throw them in wherever they're needed."

"I like that idea, Blade. A force of picked men, faithfully obeying our orders, able to keep their mouths shut—"

Blade didn't like the tone of Serana's voice or the expression on her face. "Serana, the mounted guard will be under *my* orders. I won't let it be used for any little plots you may have against the Bossirs."

"I resent—"

"You can resent my suspicions as much as you want, and I won't change my mind. I won't cooperate in any treachery against Zemun Bossir, either. If necessary, I'll ask Count Drago to help me pick the men. You may be better off, helping rule Morina for Zemun's son. I imagine you could even find ways of making sure the boy never lives to rule. But what about Morina?"

Serana's face turned very pale, and she swept out of the room without a word. Blade sighed and poured himself more wine. He knew he'd been rude, but he also suspected he'd been right. Serana might very well risk an "accident" to Zemun Bossir and trust to luck and her own wits to prevent civil war in Morina. Blade knew he was going to have to

137

keep a close watch on both of them—and also on his own back, now that he'd earned Serana's resentment. She might now be thinking of arranging an "accident" for him as well as for young Bossir.

Things would be a great deal simpler if the Wolves would only come. Then there would be enough fighting to keep everybody too busy for plotting.

Chapter 21

At last the Wolves came.

The first sign of their coming was the expected pillars of smoke on the horizon. Then came messengers from the scouting parties on sweating, half-dead heudas. Finally came the refugees.

The Wolves were approaching Morina in a great arc, thirty miles from tip to tip. As they moved they killed, raped, and destroyed. Everything they couldn't eat, drink, or carry away they smashed or burned. Houses and fields went up in flames, fruit trees were girdled, wells filled with manure or dead bodies. Behind them they left a grisly trail of ashes, rubble, and charred or gutted human bodies.

Before they fled everyone who could move, with whatever they could snatch up and sling on their own backs or the backs of their heudas. The refugees poured down the roads to Morina and swarmed around the city's gates. Blade was able to persuade some to keep on going southward, out of reach of the coming battle and hopefully out of reach of the Wolves. Many of the refugees were too mad with fear to think clearly. They saw safety behind the stout walls of Morina, and never mind that they'd be eating its food and sharing its doom if it fell.

Blade did his best to have the refugees questioned and searched as they came, but that "best" was not very good. There were too many refugees and too few men at the gates. There were other problems as well, as Zemun Bossir told Blade one morning.

"Some of the men don't seem to be interested in searching at all. They won't even shake a bag or open a box."

"Is there anything special about the men who are doing this?"

"Most of the ones I've seen are those who've been on palace duty."

"You suspect the duke?"

"It would be the logical thing for him to do—get spies or even Wolves into the city, disguised as refugees."

"Logic isn't proof."

"No, and we won't be able to prove anything. If I start questioning the men, they'll resent it and we'd just be warning the duke. I'm glad we have your mounted guard."

So was Blade. The seventy-five men of his mounted guard were now the best-trained and best-equiped fighting force in Morina. They all had good heudas, lances, bows, helmets, and axes or maces. Many of them had armor—chain mail, pulled out of secret hiding places, or improvised back and breast plates. They could do anything seventy-five men could do against any possible enemies, even the Wolves. Blade could only wish he had ten times as many of them.

Along with the refugees, messages from elsewhere in Rentoro came in almost every day. Several cities that supported the Wizard were sending their armies out to join the Wolves. Several others were sending their armies to join the defenders of Morina. Tens of thousands of men were on the march in Rentoro, a land where hardly anyone except the Wolves had raised a sword in half a century. Now the horizon was blackened with smoke in all directions, not just where the Wolves marched.

As the Wolves marched, the handful of Morinans who could fight in the open nipped at their heels, laid ambushes, cut down bridges and trees, and scouted in their rear. They killed a few Wolves and learned a good deal. Most of what they learned was encouraging.

"The Wizard has done his best to fit out the Wolves for a long campaign, but he hasn't done the job too well. They've got only a few siege engines, practically no spare animals, and only a small wagon train. They won't be able to feed themselves through a long siege. Burning over the countryside behind them won't help either."

"So what does this mean?" asked Serana.

"It means that the Wolves must either win quickly or retreat. If we can keep them out of Morina for as little as a month, we've won. Then they will have to retreat, and if they do that, many of the cities who now support the Wizard may change sides. We're the heart of the rebellion, and the

Wizard's only hope is to strike us down quickly. If he fails—"
Blade shrugged.

"Then if Duke Efrim is planning any treachery, it will be something that can help the Wolves win a quick victory," said Zemun Bossir.

"Exactly," said Blade. That didn't tell them very much, unfortunately. What he feared most was a spy smuggling in a pair of crystals, so that the Wolves could pour across a sky-bridge and emerge in the heart of Morina. They were certainly small enough to be concealed in a dozen different ways. To be sure, it took some time to tune new sky-bridge crystals for a city. But the Wizard and all of his best assistants could have been working night and day since they knew the crystals for Morina were gone.

At least Morina had alert sentries and the mounted guard to use against such a sudden eruption of Wolves. There was another danger which Blade feared even more, because there was absolutely nothing that could be done against it.

The Wizard had spoken of coming with his Wolves against Morina, to use his mental powers on the city and sow panic among the people. Was he riding with the Wolves? Would he bring all his mental powers to bear, and what would happen if he did? Would the sentries on the wall abandon their posts, the women run screaming through the streets, the fighting men cower and cringe, unable to raise a weapon to defend themselves? Blade didn't even like to think about the possibility, and he refused to mention it to any of the Morinans.

On the fifth morning after the first smoke clouds, the northern horizon came alive with gleaming helmets. A final messenger rode in, with a letter from the outlaw leader, Arno of the Mask. He was on his way south to Morina, with all his men and all those he could gather up on the way. The Morinans should be of good cheer, for his coming would surely bring them victory and good fortune.

Under other circumstances the arrogance of the message would have been amusing. As it was, the only thing that made Serana cheerful was the idea of chopping off Arno's head as soon as they'd finished with the Wolves. Blade let her fume and swear. The angrier she got at the distant Arno, the less she'd be thinking about treachery against Zemun Bossir.

Then the Wolves drew an iron circle around Morina, and for the city and everybody in it, the rest of the world no longer existed.

It was the tenth night of the siege of Morina. Blade and Zemun Bossir were walking along the walls. Both walked bent forward, to keep their heads below the top of the improvised wooden battlements. The Wolves kept archers close up to the moat, and even at night they were dangerously accurate.

It was another of those black Rentoran nights. Blade wondered if the Wolves were going to take advantage of this darkness to make their long-awaited assault on the city. They'd been building rams and scaling ladders ever since they settled into their siege camp.

He walked on, occasionally stopping to glance across the tangled rooftops of Morina toward the ducal palace. Its tall domed bell tower was the best observation point in Morina. A small force of guards picked by Count Drago kept watch from the bell chamber. Duke Efrim apparently didn't mind having them up there.

Blade wondered if the duke could still be planning any treachery, if he would let his own palace be used as an observation point. The men up there could not only watch the city and the surrounding countryside, they could keep an eye on the palace courtyards as well.

Two lanterns lit up the bell chamber. As Blade looked at the tower, he thought he saw one of them start to flicker, as if blown by a strong wind. Suddenly it went out, like a snuffed candle. A moment later the second lantern also went out. Darkness swallowed the tower, but before it did Blade could have sworn he saw a man-sized, man-shaped object plunge out into space from one of the chamber windows.

That could have been his imagination. The lanterns were something else. They couldn't have been blown out by the wind—not when Blade could barely feel the air stirring around him.

He turned and dashed back to Zemun Bossir. "Somebody's playing tricks in the ducal palace. The lanterns are out in the bell chamber."

Zemun looked and nodded. "You think?"

"I'm not going to waste time thinking, and don't you do it either. Put all the sentries on the alert and give them torches. Get the reserve archers awake and have them ready to man the walls."

"You—"

"I'm going to take the mounted guards and head for the

palace. I'll pick up the extra men I need on the way. Oh, load a dozen or so of our tar barrels into a wagon. I'll want to take them with me."

"I—"

"You'll stay here. If anything's happening at the palace, it may still be just a diversion. There could be an attack planned on the walls, if we send everybody off to the palace. So you'll stay here and take care of the walls."

Blade had forgotten he was addressing the heir-apparent of Morina and wouldn't have cared if he'd remembered. He was almost sure something was badly wrong at the palace. He was absolutely sure that if it was, minutes would be precious, and wasting time in being polite a crime.

Fortunately Zemun was too good a soldier to worry about manners in an emergency. He nodded. "I'll have them start loading the barrels at once, Lord Blade." He looked down inside the wall and opened his mouth to shout to the nearest man. Blade pulled him back and whispered fiercely in his ear.

"Don't shout yet. We don't want the whole city awake and in a panic. That could be part of the Wolves' plan."

If there was an enemy plan, thought Blade as he headed for the nearest stairs to the ground. He still couldn't be sure whether he'd be saving Morina by sounding the alert or just making a complete ass of himself. However, he could survive looking foolish better than Morina could survive an attack by the Wolves.

He went down the stairs two at a time, sprang on to his heuda's back without touching the stirrups, and galloped off toward the quarters of the mounted guards. Behind him he heard the rumble of barrels being rolled across the cobblestones and the creaking as they were loaded into the wagon. The tar barrels were intended to provide light on the walls, and also to be dropped on Wolves. Tonight they might have other uses.

During the night, the mounted guards kept their heudas saddled and ready to go. Half were always awake and the others slept in their armor with their weapons close at hand. All Blade had to do was ride up, dismount, and call softly into the guardroom. The guards came swarming out, the ones who'd been sleeping only a little behind their comrades. All seventy-five were mounted in a few minutes. Blade sent some off to alert more of Morina's defenders and led the rest toward the palace.

The streets of Morina wound and twisted, and houses with high-peaked roofs crowded close on either side. Blade caught only rare glimpses of the bell tower. The third time he saw it, the bell chamber was lit up again, more brightly than before. He watched until the roofs once more cut off his view, but saw nothing moving up there. He did see the ducal banner, now visible around one corner of the tower. It was hanging as limply as a wet handkerchief. No wind had blown out the lanterns.

The clattering hooves of the mounted guards' heudas on the cobblestones brought heads popping out of windows as they passed. Blade called out reassurances.

"Stay in your houses, everybody, and keep your doors locked. Get your weapons out if you have any, but leave things to the soldiers for the moment. We'll warn you all the moment there's any danger."

At last they came out into a slightly broader street between high-walled noblemen's houses. A hundred feet farther on, the street led them into the square in front of the ducal palace. Its walls rose thirty feet above the square, grim, ancient blocks of dark stone. The gate itself looked like a small castle. The torches burning on the gate towers, the sentries marching back and forth, helmeted heads visible above the battlements, the lights in the palace buildings beyond the wall—everything was perfectly normal.

No, not everything. At the foot of the wall lay a sprawled body. It wore the clothing of one of the palace guards, except for the helmet. The torches above cast enough light for Blade to see a dark stain on the pavement under the body.

Blade reined his heuda to a stop, and as he did the bolt from a crossbow whistled past his head. A second threw up sparks from the pavement, and a third drilled his heuda through the skull. Blade leaped clear as the dying animal toppled, landed on hands and knees, and leaped to his feet shouting orders.

Battle was joined now, and there was no more reason to be quiet. Blade roared out his orders in a voice that could be heard clear across the square. "Wolves in the palace! The duke has betrayed us! Mounted guards—back, and block the street. Get the tar barrels into a line and light them!"

His arms danced wildly. "You—ride to Lord Zemun. Tell him to get the torches lit and man the walls.

"You—ride back to the men coming up behind us. Send

them around to block all the streets leading out from the palace. Have them use wagons, furniture, barrels, tear up the cobblestones if they have to. We've got to surround the palace and keep it surrounded!"

More bolts sailed down from the gate to punctuate Blade's remarks. One struck a guard in the arm, nearly knocking him out of his saddle. He cried out, but with surprise and rage more than pain.

"You, you, you—ride through the streets and wake up the people. Tell them the Wolves are in the city and must be stopped. Tell them to turn out, block the streets, light torches and be ready to fight for their lives." Blade's mind went back to Winston Churchill's call of 1940, when Britain faced a German invasion. "Remember, you can always take one with you."

The messengers clattered off into the darkness on their various missions, pursued by more bolts from the gate. The rest dismounted, some to lead away the heudas, others to unload the tar barrels and pile them across the street. Still others broke down the doors of nearby houses and started dragging furniture out into the street to add to the barricade. At first men shouted angrily at the invasion of their homes. Then they heard what was happening and came swarming out to join the mounted guards at the barricade.

They came in their nightclothes or in no clothes at all. Some came with axes and spears, others with improvised clubs, chair legs, or even stones. Some climbed up to top-floor windows and got ready to throw things down on the heads of the Wolves. None of them seemed to have any idea of how to fight a battle except killing all the Wolves they could find. Blade had seldom commanded a stranger or more ragged army, but he'd never commanded one as eager to fight!

Now Blade could hear a growing uproar behind the walls of the palace. Heudas stamped and cried out, men shouted orders, a rumble of voices rose and fell. The Wolves were gathering there in strength, but they seemed to be taking their time about coming out to attack. Blade wondered if they despised the Morinans that much. Surely they could see the barricades rising all around the palace! Did they think they had all night?

Then silence fell behind the palace walls. In the next moment the main gate crashed open. In the moment after that what seemed like a thousand Wolves came charging out of the palace on their heudas.

At the head of the column was a mass of leaders in full armor, riding almost shoulder to shoulder, their lances raised, pennons fluttering, armor gleaming in the torchlight. They cantered out into the square, the lances dipped, and the whole mass came thundering down on Blade's force. They were a terrifying sight—a massed charge by armored heavy cavalry always is. As he dashed forward with a torch to ignite the tar barrels, Blade wondered if he'd be alone when he turned around.

The torch fell, the tar blazed up, and a wall of flame rose between Blade and the charging Wolves. He dashed back for the cover of the barricade, vaulted it, and shouted to his men, "Men with spears and lances—line up and hold them out in front of you. The rest—gather on the flanks and the rear. No prisoners!"

Then the Wolves reached the wall of flame, and Blade stopped shouting because he could no longer make himself heard.

The Wolves tried hard to rein in and stay out of the flames. But the first rank, the second, and some of the third were too close, and the sheer weight of their comrades behind them pushed them into the fire. Men and heudas came down like falling trees, and all the screams blended together into one ghastly uproar.

Blade saw a Wolf leader plunge to the ground at his feet and start to get up. Then a pain-maddened heuda reared above him and brought both front hooves down on his chest. The armor caved in like tinfoil and the man died writhing and gasping, unable to cry out.

Another Wolf landed face down in the thickest of the burning tar. By some miracle he got to his feet and came lurching toward Blade, flames shooting out from the chinks of his armor as the tar ate away his flesh, screaming with every step he took. Three spears jabbed the man in the chest, knocking him over. Blade knelt over the fallen man and thrust his dagger through the eyeslit of the helmet to end the screaming.

A man in a nightshirt seemed to go mad, rushing past the line of spears waving an ax. His clothing caught fire, but he kept on, straight into the middle of the Wolves. "For Magra, for Magra, for Magra!" he howled, as the flames charred his flesh and the Wolves' swords bit into it. Then his ax came down, sweeping a man-at-arms out of the saddle, and both fell dead. Magra was avenged.

Dead or dying men and heudas piled up along the wall of flame, writhing and twisting, filling the air with screams and the overpowering stench of burning flesh. A few of the men-at-arms unlimbered crossbows and sent stray bolts whistling into the ranks of the defenders. The archers were shooting blind, though, and did little damage.

At last the bodies piled up high enough to make a clear path through the flames at one end. The Wolves turned toward it, found they could not force their heudas over the bodies, drew back, and milled around, apparently uncertain what to do next. Blade wished he had about fifty archers, and thought of sending a message to ask for some from the walls. He decided against it. The Wolves here made a tempting target, but it was still too soon to risk stripping the walls.

As he watched the Wolves milling around, a suspicion grew in Blade's mind and slowly turned into a certainty. The Wizard was not here. Perhaps he was not in the besieging army at all, but certainly he was nowhere within sight of this force of Wolves. He was not seeing what was going on, either by view-ball or with his own eyes. So he could not give them any orders. Without the orders they'd always had from their master, the orders that had so often saved them from having to think for themselves, the Wolf leaders could not lead. Without the Wizard the Wolves might not be toothless, but they certainly seemed witless. They could march, burn a countryside, set up a siege camp. They could not fight a pitched battle against opponents who fought back, thought for themselves, and could spring sudden surprises!

It was hard for Blade to believe anything else. The Wizard had fought in many battles, or at least knew how they should be fought. If he'd been giving orders to these Wolves, they would not have waited so long to come out of the palace. They would not have charged blindly straight at the wall of flame and a barricade that might conceal anything. They would not be milling around now like a flock of sheep without a leader.

Morina was going to win.

"Morina will win!" Blade roared. "Morina will win! The Wizard does not lead the Wolves, and they cannot lead themselves! Stand, men of Morina, and from this night on you

147

will be the masters of the Wizard's Wolves! Stand, kill, and be free!"

"Stand!"

"Kill the Wolves!"

"This is the night of our freedom!"

The cries rose behind Blade, until they were as loud as the screams had been. The surviving Wolf leaders started scrambling down from their heudas, shouting to the men-at-arms to do the same. Holding their lances out in front of them like pikes, the leaders began crowding across the piled bodies, the men-at-arms behind them.

Now the Wolves' archers could no longer fire without risk of hitting their own comrades. A messenger ran up to Blade and shouted in his ear. The other streets were all barricaded; did the Lord Blade wish some of the men there to come around to meet the Wolves here?

"No. We can hold them for the time being. Stay where you are. You'll have your share of fighting before the night's over, don't worry."

The messenger dashed off. Blade sheathed his sword and bent to pick up an intricately engraved battle ax, fallen from the hand of a Wolf leader. He raised it high and the light of the burning tar flamed across the polished blue steel.

"Men of Morina!" he shouted, and then another rallying cry from Home Dimension's warfare sprang to his mind. "Men of Morina! *They shall not pass!*" Blade whirled the ax over his head, then sent it whining toward the shaft of a Wolf's lance. The lance split in two, the point rang on the cobblestones, and Blade sprang into the gap it left to close with the Wolf.

The Wolf leaders were fully armored and Blade was not. With both sides on foot that was an advantage for Blade. The Wolf leaders had to move eighty pounds of steel with every step they took. Blade carried less than a third that much. He stormed through the ranks of the Wolf leaders as though he was the Wolf and they the sheep. His ax whirled, whined, and smashed down with sparks, the clang of splitting armor, and the indescribable sounds of shattering bones and tearing flesh.

The Wolf leaders tried to surround blade, but the gap was so narrow and they were so tightly packed together he could block them completely. One Wolf leader did get around Blade, tried to stab him in the back, and was promptly attacked by five Morinans. His mace smashed two of them into the ground, then the others drove him into the barricade. He fell over a jutting chair leg, fell back into an upturned table, and the other three men swarmed over him. He knocked another down with his mace, but the last two got up again and he did not.

Blade held the Wolf leaders at bay single-handedly for a good five minutes. Finally the pile of armored bodies widened the gap in the flames until he could no longer hold it by himself. The Wolves poured through, to be met head-on by the mounted guards and by Morinans who had too much to avenge to be worried about such a minor thing as their own lives. The Wolf leaders were good fighters, each worth two or three Morinans, and their armor protected them from much. They were not good enough or well-protected enough to stand agaist people who only wanted to kill and didn't care about being killed in the process.

So the fight exploded all along the barricade, with Blade in the middle of it, still swinging his ax. At last the press of bodies around him grew so thick he no longer had room to swing. He drew his dagger and began stabbing Wolves through the eyeslits of their helmets, under their armpits, anywhere their armor offered him a vulnerable point. He stabbed again and again, until his dagger was coated an inch deep in congealed blood and began to lose its point. He lost track of how the battle was going, how many of his own men and how many Wolves were dead, even how many men he'd killed himself.

Suddenly the whistle of arrows and bolts was added to the uproar, followed by screams as they struck into the ranks of the men-at-arms behind the Wolf leaders. Other arrows struck the Wolves' heudas. The maddened animals jerked themselves free of the men-at-arms holding them and bolted in all directions. A man-at-arms tried to stop one and the desperate animal drove one of its sharp horns into his thigh. The man was lifted high, screaming and thrashing, then dropped to the ground where a dozen more heudas trampled him.

Blade looked up and saw the windows and roofs of the houses on either side of the street crammed with archers. Zemun Bossir must have decided that it was worth stripping the walls, if the Wolves' attack from the palace could be smashed quickly. Well, they could argue the point in the morning, if they both lived through the night. The Wolves weren't going

149

to get through along this street, but that didn't mean the fight was over. There were four other streets, all of them had to be held, and there could still be an assault on the walls. The Wolves might even learn how to fight a battle on their own!

Blade was still on his feet when dawn broke over Morina, after one of the longest and bloodiest nights of his life. The Wolves kept coming out of the palace and hurling themselves at the barricades. Blade rode from one danger point to another, rallying the defenders against each successive attack.

"They shall not pass!" The cry that rallied the French defenders of Verdun in 1916 now rallied the Morinans against the Wolves. The improvised barricades of furniture and cobblestones were held as firmly as if they'd been walls of solid iron.

After a while, the Wolves gave up trying to crack the barricades and tried to outflank them. Then there was more savage fighting, house-to-house and even room-to-room. Blade himself grappled with a Wolf leader and threw him down a flight of stairs. His armor did not save him from a three-story fall. Other Wolves died with their faces smashed in by chunks of firewood, were scalded by boiling water, were pushed into fireplaces filled with hot coals.

When the Wolves could choose their ground, they were as good as ever. Then four or five Morinans would die for every Wolf. But the Wolves were not often that lucky, and even certain death did not stop the Morinans. They quickly sensed they had the advantage, and became more fearless and more bloodthirsty as the night went on.

Twice the Wolves in the camp outside Morina tried an attack on the city walls. The first time the archers were busy inside the city, so the Wolves were able to cross the moat and get a foothold on the walls. Then Zemun Bossir led a counterattack with every man he could scrape together and drove the Wolves back.

After that Blade ordered all the archers back to the wall. "If I see one of you anywhere else tonight, I'll strangle him with my own hands." The archers obeyed, and when the Wolves came on the second time they were beaten off more easily. The tar barrels gave the archers plenty of light, and even women and children helped push down scaling ladders.

The Wolves continued their attacks until the sky began to turn gray. Then they seemed to accept their defeat and began a slow, stubborn retreat toward the palace. There lay the crystals of the sky-bridge that had brought them in and now would take them out again in safety.

They never crossed the sky-bridge. Duke Efrim's household guards had been willing to let the Wolves in, hoping to be spared along with their master after the Wizard's victory. Now they saw defeat hanging over the Wolves and doom hanging over them. The people of Morina would tear them and their master to shreds long before the Wizard could do anything to save them.

So they turned against the Wolves. The retreating men found arrows hitting them in the back. Those who reached the palace found the gates locked against them. Most of the Wolves died in a final, desperate hand-to-hand struggle under the walls of the palace, attacked on all sides. Blade managed to have a few spared as prisoners for questioning. Then the duke's guards opened the palace gates and the people of Morina swarmed in, howling for Duke Efrim's blood.

They did not get it. Blade and Serana found the duke lying on the floor of the bell chamber, an empty wine cup clutched in one hand. He'd taken a dose of the same poison he'd used on so many of his and the Wizard's enemies.

Blade saw that the duke's wife and children were escorted out of the palace and turned over to Haymi Razence. The innkeeper seemed to be keeping his head. His personal guards could be trusted to keep their prisoners out of sight and safe from the mob.

With the duke accounted for, the search for the sky-bridge crystals began. It ended swiftly and spectacularly. The crystals must have been active when they were found, and whoever tried to smash them wasn't as lucky as Blade. The explosion flattened a whole wing of the palace and buried most of the duke's personal servants in the rubble. "Good riddance to the whole lot," was Serana's epitaph for them.

By Serana's orders, Duke Efrim's body was placed on one of the new stone-throwers and hurled over the walls, to tell the Wolves that Morina was no longer vulnerable to treachery. His head was cut off and stuck on a spike over the main gate of the palace.

Blade was increasingly glad he would not be staying in Morina after the end of the fighting. Serana was a lovely and gifted woman, but there was a bloodthirsty streak in her that Blade was coming to like less and less. He didn't blame her for having it, not after all she'd been through, but he didn't want to find himself in its path either.

Count Drago Bossir had an arrow wound in his thigh, which was almost a relief to Blade. The wound wouldn't kill the old man, but it would keep him out of the rest of the fighting. Blade found himself increasingly determined that Count Drago should live to see the breaking of the Wizard's power and the destruction of the Wolves who had done so much to him.

Zemun Bossir, on the other hand, had come through all the fighting unwounded, covering himself with glory and other people's blood. If Serana was laying any plots against him, she hadn't been able to do anything. Perhaps that would discourage her.

When all the bodies were counted up, there were more than six hundred dead Wolves, a third of them leaders. That was a loss the Wolves could not afford. There were also more than two thousand dead Morinans, a loss the city couldn't afford. The battle had been a bloody mess; the next battle would be even worse.

Morina would get no reinforcements, but neither would the Wolves. Blade learned that from the Wolf prisoners. The armies of cities friendly to Morina would never break through the Wolves, but they were keeping the armies of cities friendly to the Wizard from coming to join the siege.

Even better news from the prisoners was that the Wizard himself was not with the army. He'd sent two-thirds of his Wolves—four thousand of them—against Morina, but as far as anyone knew he hadn't left his castle since the rebellion began.

Blade was relieved. Now there was no danger of the Wizard's mental powers sowing panic and terror in Morina. He could send messages to individual men over great distances, but not terrorize thirty-five thousand people.

Almost as important, his own job would be easier, once the Wolves were defeated. Behind the walls of his castle, the Wizard was safe from the Rentorans, who would gladly cut him into small pieces with dull knives. Whether he would consider returning to Home Dimension with Blade, after Blade had led the Rentorans in smashing his power, was another question. At least the Wizard would be alive for Blade to ask him, and that was something. Blade wasn't particularly optimistic about getting the Wizard back to Home Dimension alive and sane, but he knew he had to try.

Freeing Rentoro from the Wizard's grip was a great accomplishment, but it could not do as much for Britain as the Wizard's secrets.

Chapter 22

Now all at once it was summer. One blazing hot day followed another. The moat with its load of dead Wolves, the garbage heaps in the back streets of Morina, the latrine pits in the enemy's camp—all sent up into the windless air a smell that grew worse with each passing day.

The smell itself didn't worry Blade. What did worry him was the possibility of disease that smell implied. Thirty-five thousand people were now crammed inside walls that normally held twenty thousand. The wells and streams provided barely enough water for drinking, none at all for washing. Filth and garbage normally carted off to fertilize nearby fields was piling higher and higher. The Wolves could not break the spirit of Morina's defenders, but a plague might.

Of course a plague could also sweep through the ranks of the Wolves. But the Wolves could ride away if they had to, seeking clean air and water, leaving behind their own filth. The Morinans had nowhere to go.

Blade had other worries beside the growing risk of plague. Count Drago was not recovering from his wound. Instead he grew weaker and weaker each day, the flesh melting from his already lean frame. An infection that Rentoro's medicine could not handle was eating him away from within.

The count didn't lack the will to live—in fact, he would have insisted on being carried to the walls each day on a litter if Blade hadn't forbidden it. It was his strength that faded steadily, and the hot, foul air of Morina didn't help. Blade had the count established in the best-ventilated room of the late Duke Efrim's palace, but that was all he could do for the old man.

The count might still live to see the final battle against the Wolves. They were hard at work in their camp, night and day, preparing for the all-out attack on the walls of Morina. Some people in Morina were allowing themselves to hope the

Wolves had lost their old spirit and the attack would be feeble. It was true that without the Wizard's leadership, they were under a great handicap. The failure of the night attack through the palace had killed off too many of the best Wolves and given the rest an unpleasant shock. They were suffering from the heat, from lack of food, and from lack of experience in camping out.

None of these things kept the Wolves from working like galley slaves. They built rams, they built massive stone-throwers, they built two tall siege towers. They piled up tons of brush to fill the moat and long planks to cross it. By night they dug trenches close to the moat, so their archers could fire from cover at the men on the walls.

The attack would come and there would be nothing feeble about it when it came. The Wolves might have the supplies and equipment for only one attack, but they would put everything they had into that one. Morina might destroy the Wolves, but it might be destroyed itself in the process, burying its enemies under its own ruins and under the piled bodies of its own people.

Blade would have won some other way if he could, but now there might be no other way.

Even Serana seemed to be caught up in the tension. For days on end she never mentioned Zemun Bossir. She cut her hair short, so that it would fit under a helmet and practiced with a sword several hours each day. She lost weight and the dark circles grew under her eyes until she looked the same as when she'd been the Wizard's prisoner.

Blade awoke in the darkness, knowing that something was wrong without being sure quite how he knew. He slipped out of bed without waking the sleeping Serana and went to the window.

It gave him a view toward the Wolves' siege camp. It lay almost invisible in the night, silent and unnaturally dark, the usual scattering of campfires gone.

The campfires were out! The Wolves had darkened their camp, and they could only be doing that to conceal something. Blade ran back to the bed and shook Serana awake. She sat up, naked and still half asleep, rubbing her eyes.

"Get up and get dressed," he said briskly. "The Wolves have darkened their camp. They may not be attacking tonight, but something's up!"

155

Serana hurried to the window to look for herself. As she did, Blade heard the tramping of feet in the street below. He wasn't the only man in Morina who thought the Wolves might be up to something.

They were pulling on their armor when Blade heard several new sounds, in a ragged chorus. There was a creaking, a groaning, and a squealing, all of it faint and wavering, as though it came from far away—beyond the walls of Morina. As Blade was buckling on his boots, fists pounded on the door, Serana drew the bolt, and one of Zemun's officers practically fell into the room.

"Lord Zemun wishes you to come to the east wall, my lord and lady," he gasped. "The Wolves are moving up their siege machines. He also says the watchers on the bell tower have seen the fires of another camp, far to the north."

More Wolves, thought Blade. The Wizard must have stripped even his castle to reinforce the attack on Morina. He wasn't going to get the victory he was hoping for, even then. Morina would eat all the Wolves he could send against it, but this would do the Morinans no good. They would buy freedom for Rentoro with their own lives and their own city. It was hard for Blade to remember that the fall of Morina would also mean his own death. Perhaps, when all was said and done, it was not so important that he'd reached the end of his road.

Blade and Serana followed the young officer down the stairs. As they reached the street a sudden *wsssh* of disturbed air sounded overhead, growing rapidly louder. It ended abruptly in a tearing crash, as something large plunged out of the sky and through the roof of a nearby house. The crackle of breaking timbers and the crash and rattle of falling masonry went on for quite a while. Before it stopped, another stone struck farther off, nearer to the walls, and then a third.

Serana started to run, but Blade held her back. "They've started the stone-throwers, but I think they're just trying to soften us up. Smash houses, kill people, block the streets, start a panic." He called to the officer. "Message for Lord Zemun. Turn out all the soldiers and have them get everybody out of the houses near the east wall. Also, have our own stone-throwers hold their fire and pull back out of range.

"It's going to be grim," he said to Serana. "But I don't think there's any danger until they start on the walls, trying to open

156

breaches for their storming parties. If we don't panic, they can't do us much harm by knocking down houses."

Serana did not reply. Her lips were moving too busily, in silent prayers to the governing Fates and whatever other gods or powers she worshipped.

The stones crashed down into Morina all the rest of the night. Blindly and impartially, they smashed houses, shops, and people in the streets. If the soldiers hadn't taken charge of the situation, the panic the Wolves hoped for might have started.

Blade, Zemun Bossir, and Serana put their men to work. Within half an hour no one in Morina was asleep. In another hour all the houses within range of the enemy's stone-throwers were empty. In all the streets along the east wall of Morina, there were only soldiers, building barricades from the rubble and standing ready to put out any fires.

Shortly after dawn there was a lull in the bombardment. From the walls, Blade could see all the Wolves' siege machines lined up across the moat, just out of bowshot. The two towers and the three battering rams were in position, ready to be pushed through the gaps in the enemy's trenches and up to the moat. Around them stood the wagons of piled brush and planks for crossing the moat.

Zemun peered through a knothole in the arrow-scarred battlements, then turned to Blade. "Lord Blade, what about bringing up our throwers and trying to hit those machines? A tar barrel or two would be the end of those towers."

Blade shook his head. "Not yet. Wait until they're up so close to the walls that the Wolves won't be able to use their own throwers. Then we can shoot without being shot at."

"But they have only a few machines. If—"

"So do we," put in Blade. "And we can't replace them as easily as the Wolves can."

Zemun frowned and seemed ready to go on arguing, when suddenly the *crunk* of a stone-thrower at work floated across from the enemy's camp. Right behind the sound came a large rock, to crash into the wall fifty yards to Blade's right. Dust rose in a cloud and he could feel the ancient stones shudder under his feet.

Here we go, thought Blade. Aloud, he said, "Get some of the archers up into the houses just behind the wall. Have them keep out of sight. The Wolves will be coming at us in

157

four or five places at once, so we can't hope to keep them all out. With archers in the houses and the barricades in the streets, the ones who get in still won't get far."

The young nobleman nodded. As he did, another stone crashed into the wall, a hundred yards to the left. This one cleaned off several yards of the wooden battlements, and Blade heard screams from the streets below as men were struck down by the falling wreckage.

All morning and into the afternoon, the stone-throwers of the Wizard's army hammered at the walls of Morina. Those walls were massive, but they were also old. They hadn't been maintained very well, either—the Wizard didn't encourage his subjects to keep their walls strong. Under the steady pounding, the walls began to give. In one place an open breach gaped, half-choked with fallen stones but still passable for men on foot. Blade had cartloads of stone and tar barrels pulled into position all around the breach, but there was nothing else to do.

The day was at its hottest when the bombardment finally stopped. The dust cloud hanging over the walls slowly drifted away on the faint breeze. Behind the walls the Morinans finished oiling and sharpening their weapons, tightened their helmet straps, and drank some water. Everyone was hungry, but no one could force himself to swallow a single bite.

Then the creak and squeal of ungreased wheels rose and the siege towers and battering rams lurched forward. The towers swayed like the masts of a ship in a storm, while the battering rams came on steadily, looking like centipedes as the hundred Wolves under each wooden cover tramped along.

At least two thousand Wolves were advancing on the walls of Morina, but only about half of them would be actually fighting. The others were pushing the towers, the rams, and the wagonloads of material for crossing the moat. A thousand Wolves might not be too many to handle.

Now there were creakings and squealings from behind Blade, to echo the ones in front. The Morinan stone-throwers were coming forward, getting into striking range. Blade lay flat on his stomach on top of the wall, estimating distances. Another few yards and the siege towers would be good targets.

Trumpets blared and drums rattled and thundered all along the line of the advancing Wolves. On top of the towers men frantically waved the wolf's-head banners. The next moment everyone was surging toward the wall like an incoming tide, and the moment after that they were in range of the Morinan stone-throwers.

Blade sprang to his feet, waving his ax, signaling frantically to the lookouts for the stone-throwers. He saw them reply, then started signalling to the men who'd been waiting out the bombardment of the wall. They scrambled up the inner face of the wall on ladders and dashed out of the battered houses. Most carried bows, all carried axes or spears.

A stone came arching up out of the city, flew over the wall, and dropped into the moat. Muddy water spouted high, drenching a dozen Wolves and making them dance and swear. Blade laughed. A second stone fell more accurately, missing one of the advancing rams by feet. Then Blade could no longer keep track of the fall of each stone, as the attack reached the walls of Morina.

The wagons of brush and planks came up to the moat, and the archers on the walls opened fire on them. Dozens of Wolves fell as they tried to manhandle long planks and huge bundles of brushwood into place. The archers supporting them fired back, and men fell from the top of the wall. The planks slammed down, and shouting Wolves ran across the rickety bridges, some carrying scaling ladders. Behind these men the brushwood slowly piled up, filling the moat.

Now the rams came on at a run. The man guiding one didn't keep his mind on the job. The ram dashed up to the moat and kept right on going, plunging the leading bearers into the filthy water. They floundered, screaming and choking as they tried to get free of the ram. Slowly and with a horrible inevitability, it tilted forward, pushing them under like a giant hand. The screams and the choking died away, and only a few bubbles came up from under the submerged end of the ram. The bearers at the other end, luckier than their comrades, scrambled out from under the wooden cover and joined the men crossing on the planks.

The other two rams came up to the most where the brushwood offered them a safe crossing. This did one of them no good. The first bearers were just stepping on to the brushwood when a heavy stone crashed down on the wooden cover. Splinters and planks flew, men screamed, and the ram stopped. Then the bearers began scrambling out from underneath. Blade saw the lucky hit had snapped most of the ropes supporting the iron-headed wooden beam of the ram, letting it sag and break in two. The whole machine was now so much useless lumber.

The third ram was the only one to reach the wall. The iron head began crunching against a section of already cracked stones. Blade could see large chunks coming loose and tumbling down to the ground, or bouncing off the wooden cover. The men on this ram seemed to be tougher than their comrades, and they kept at their work.

Those men would get through, Blade realized. He could only hope the men at the barricades and the archers in the houses could hold them. He had too much to do here on the wall. On either side of him the heads of scaling ladders were sprouting, then the armored heads of Wolf leaders. One rose almost at Blade's feet, turning from side to side as if the man was trying to get his bearings. Blade brought his ax down on the helmet as hard as he could. The Wolf leader threw up his hands and toppled backward off the wall, taking three comrades and the ladder with him.

Another ladder rose beside Blade. He kicked at it and saw it fall backward. The Wolves on it leaped clear and landed safely—for a moment. Two archers fired down at them and one Wolf sprawled on the ground, writhing and kicking until he writhed himself into the moat. The fighting was now so mixed up that the Wolf archers on the ground could not fire safely. The Morinans had no such problem. Anyone coming at them across the ground outside the wall was an enemy, and often a fine target as well.

Another ladder, and another, and a third. The man on the first ladder had his visor open and Blade's ax split apart his sweating face. Blade was turning to the second ladder when someone drove a spear down between it and the wall, then heaved. The man on top of the ladder slashed at the spearman, laying open his unarmored stomach. He gasped and put all his strength into a last desperate heave. The ladder went over backward with a chorus of screams, then the dying spearman toppled off the wall and landed on top of his victims.

Blade was about to attack the third ladder when he heard a gruesome chorus of screams from beyond the moat. Blazing tar from a well-aimed barrel was covering the top of a siege tower with a crown of flames and dripping down the sides. The Wolves hadn't taken the precaution of wetting down the tower's sides or covering them with leather. It was going up like a pile of kindling. Blade saw writhing bodies among the flames on the top, and saw others jump, hair and clothing aflame. He also heard more screams from those unlucky enough to be inside the tower and unable to get out. They went on screaming for quite a while, until one side of the tower cracked open like an eggshell. Flames roared up, curling around the blackening timbers and mercifully drowning out the last of the screams.

With other men than the Wizard's Wolves, Blade might have expected the burning of the tower to be the end of the attack. Few men would come on unshaken by seeing and hearing their comrades roasted alive. But the Wolves were fighting not only for victory but for their own lives. It was kill or be killed for both sides.

So the Wolves came on. A column marched toward the breach in the wall and started scrambling up the tumbled blocks. The footing on the loose stones was so precarious that the leaders in their heavy armor could not climb. The men-at-arms scrambled up, some falling with arrows in them, others pushed back by spears, a few simply losing their balance. Some got through—and then a vast cloud of smoke billowed up, as tar barrels were ignited in their faces. Blade sent a messenger off with orders to the stone-thrower crews, to aim one of their machines at the breach and keep it firing as fast as they could.

Now the second siege tower was crossing the moat. It wobbled and swayed drunkenly as it crossed the precarious bridge of planks on top of brushwood. The archers on top ceased firing, too busy hanging on for dear life. Then the tower was rumbling steadily toward the wall. A tar barrel came smoking down from the sky and Blade held his breath, hoping it would land on the tower. The barrel bounced off the side of the tower, scattering flaming tar over the dead and wounded, then rolled into the moat in a cloud of steam.

Blade could now see where the siege tower was going to reach the wall. The archers on top were firing again and the Wolves on the ground were crowding around. The men on top were pushing out a heavy wooden plank. It swayed in the air as it reached for the wall.

Blade started running toward where the plank would drop. He saw Zemun Bossir running toward the same place from the opposite position. Arrows and bolts whistled around the young nobleman as he ran, but none of them hit him.

161

"No!" Blade shouted. "We shouldn't both be here, you young idiot! Get back!"

If Zemun heard Blade's shouts, he ignored them. There seemed to be a battle-madness in him, that made him totally indifferent to the world around him. No, that wasn't quite true. The wild eyes in the grimy faced were fixed on the siege tower as if it had some hypnotic attraction. Zemun stopped, waved his sword, shouted curses, ignored more bolts and arrows—then the heavy plank swayed one final time and crashed down on top of him. Even over the uproar of the battle, Blade heard Zemun Bossir's skull crack.

Blade covered the rest of the distance to the plank so quickly that he was there before the first Wolf crossed it. Blade met that unfortunate Wolf, his ax swinging in both hands. The man flew off the plank and landed very nearly in two pieces. The second man was a Wolf leader. Blade smashed his shield with one swing, his shoulder with a second, his face with a third. The Wolf leader collapsed on top of the wall, falling almost beside Zemun Bossir.

Blade killed three more Wolves with his ax, then the handle cracked. He grappled a fourth man with his bare hands and heaved him backward into his comrades so that three of them fell off the plank. More Wolves scrambled up into the tower from the ground, but by now Morina's defenders were swarming up to meet them. Now Blade was in the middle of a swirling hand-to-hand combat where men hacked, kicked, and thrust at each other, and threw each other off the wall when they couldn't do anything else.

Suddenly the Wolves stopped coming across the plank. Blade snatched up a fallen mace and ran across the plank to the top of the tower. A Wolf leader's head poked up through the hole in the wooden floor, and Blade's mace crashed down on it. Then three Morinans ran up along the wall, carrying a huge iron hook tied to a hundred feet of heavy rope. They tossed the hook to Blade, who swung it down and drove it firmly into a joint in the floor under him. Then he ran back to the wall and threw the plank down. Every man who could grab the rope did so, someone started a chant, and the men began to pull. As more Wolves scrambled out on top of the tower, it swayed farther than ever before, hung precariously for a second, then went over with a crash. The Wolves on top jumped, but misjudged their distance. They landed safely, but a second later the falling tower landed on top of them, mashing them into the ground. Blade called for torches and tar barrels to burn the tower, then ran back along the wall to his former position.

Blade alternated between being a fighter and being a general all the rest of the afternoon, because the Wolves went on attacking as if they still had some hope of winning. Blade couldn't see how they could believe this, with so much of their siege equipment smashed and the Morinans still holding as firm as ever. Were they hoping for the Wizard to come to their aid, or did they perhaps hope the Morinans' courage might still crack? Certainly there seemed to be no end to the Wolves, so the reinforcements from the north had probably arrived.

Afterward, Blade couldn't have told a coherent story of the rest of the afternoon's fighting for a million pounds. It was just one endless slaughter, the Wolves coming on, the Morinans holding, and the men on both sides dying. There were times when Blade wondered if perhaps he'd died and gone to Hell. It was hard to believe there could be this much blood, this much killing, this many screams of pain and rage anywhere else.

Blade did know that in time the attacks came to an end. No more Wolves stormed forward over the heaped bodies of their comrades. No more bolts plucked men off the wall beside Blade. From inside the city he could hear the sounds of minor skirmishing. The mounted guards and bands of civilians under Haymi Razence were hunting down the last Wolves who'd managed to get past the walls. There weren't many of those Wolves left, and the sounds of the fighting were scattered and faint.

In fact, there weren't going to be many Wolves left anywhere. Blade didn't know how many men this day's fighting had left dead or maimed, and he couldn't even force his numbed brain to make a guess. He did know that Morina had given the Wolves a second hammering, and from this one they could never recover. The armies of Rentoro would now outnumber the Wolves eight or ten to one. With that kind of odds in their favor, they could march out and meet the Wolves in the open field. No more Rentoran cities would have to stand these murderous sieges, see their women and children crushed under falling houses, and have their cobblestones turn dark with blood.

Blade was just getting used to the relative silence that was falling over the city, when suddenly it came apart all over again. There was a frantic boiling of movement all around the Wolves' camp, with men on foot and men on heudas dashing about. No two of them seemed to be moving in the same direction. Some of the riders went down, others trampled Wolves under the hooves of their mounts. A vast cloud of dust rose as the Wolves' heudas stampeded, and the thunder of their stampede drowned out all the other sounds.

Suddenly Blade realized what was happening. He sprinted to the nearest stairs, plunged down them to the street, and ran to the nearest saddled heuda he could find. He vaulted into the saddle and wrenched the animal's head toward the nearest gate, just as Serana ran up. She was in hacked and dust-covered armor, and there was blood on one cheek and on the sword she waved.

"Someone's attacking the Wolves' camp!" Blade shouted. "I have to ride out there and find out who's leading them!" He waved his mace at the gate guards. "Pull those wagons clear, now! Move!"

The wagons blocking the gate rumbled aside, the gate creaked open, and Blade spurred his heuda up to a gallop. He pounded through the gate, leaving Serana staring open-mouthed after him. He was glad to have an excuse not to talk to her. She'd done her share of the fighting and certainly nothing about Zemun Bossir's death could be blamed on her. Still, the deaths of both Count Drago and his grandson would make the succession of the Bossirs in Morina complicated, to say the least. Blade didn't want to say anything about the matter to anyone until he had time to put his own thoughts in order and find out who was out there, joining Morina's battle at the last moment.

Blade thundered out of the gate and crossed the moat on one of the Wolves' piles of brushwood and planks. He passed several small clusters of Wolves. They stood watching him in numb silence, like men who'd been hit over the head but hadn't found time to fall down. Blade did see one Wolf leader topple over as he passed, a man apparently quite unwounded. Sunstroke, probably. The Wolf leaders had been fighting all day under a broiling hot sun, encased in full plate armor.

By the time Blade came up behind the Wolf camp, most of the heudas were long gone and the dust cloud was settling. The mounted men were riding about, chasing those Wolves who hadn't run off after their mounts. Some of the Wolves were trying to surrender, and a few of them were actually succeeding.

The mounted men were mostly small, wiry types, in weather-stained dark clothing, mounted on thin, nervous heudas. "Where's your leader?" Blade called out.

One of them jerked a thumb after the fleeing heudas. "Gone t'run down Wolves."

Blade spent a frustrating couple of hours trying to catch up with the leader of the new arrivals. Three times he reached the place of a battle just after the fighting ended and the leader rode off after more Wolves. It was getting dark and Blade was several miles from Morina before he finally caught up with the man.

The leader was a man about the same size and shape as Zemun Bossir. He sat on his heuda as if he and the animal were a single body, and his entire face was covered by a black leather mask. Blade realized this must be the leader of the northern outlaws, Arno of the Mask. Well, the man had said he was riding south to help Morina. He'd also said he'd guarantee them victory. In a way he had—the Wolves wouldn't even be able to make a safe retreat with their heudas driven off. But Arno and his men would be wise not to claim too much credit. After all their losses, the Morinans would not much care for that.

Blade introduced himself. "I am Lord Blade, the commander of the fighting men of Morina. You are Arno?"

"I am." The voice also resembled Zemun Bossir's. "Do you wish me to come to the city with you?"

"Yes."

"I can do that. My captains will be able to deal with the last of the Wolves."

It was nearly dark when they rode up to the walls of Morina, but there was plenty of man-made light. The walls were lined with cheering Morinans, waving torches and candles, and outside each gate a tar barrel spewed flame. Blade and Arno rode in, and waited as Serana and a dozen of the mounted guards rode out to meet them.

As Serana rode up, Arno looked on either side of him and behind him, as if to make sure no one was lurking there. Then he raised both hands to his mask, and stripped it off. Blade was surprised that the face underneath was not at all deformed.

165

Blade's surprise was nothing compared to Serana's. She took one look at Arno's face—then her face turned white under the blood and grime, and her mouth sagged open. She swayed, and for a moment Blade was certain she was going to tumble out of the saddle in a faint.

Then she closed her mouth and said, in a voice that was half a gasp, "Nebon Bossir! You?"

The man who'd called himself Arno of the Mask smiled and nodded.

"But you—you're dead!"

"No. It turned out that I could run fast enough to escape from the Wolves, then lead outlaws well enough to keep the Wolves at a distance. Now I have come home. We let our fires show last night, in the hope of drawing the Wolves off from you, but I see we could not. Well, they are dead one way or another." He threw his mask to the ground. "How is my brother? And is my grandfather still alive?"

Blade realized with a shock that he'd completely forgotten to tell Nebon anything about Morina's fighting. Fatigue must have driven out the last of his wits! "Your brother Zemun was killed, leading our men in this day's fighting. Your grandfather still lives, but he is dying of an arrow wound received when Duke Efrim's treachery let the Wolves into the city."

Blade tried to sum up the fighting in a few sentences. Before he was halfway through, he realized Nebon was hardly listening.

"I must go in and see my grandfather," he said. "Is the city safe?"

"The Wolves who entered are dead or prisoners," said Serana, forcing a smile. "We shall welcome your return."

"Yes," said Blade. "But I don't think you should enter the city until you've got a few of your own men as an escort. There are some in Morina who are of two minds about the House of Bossir."

Serana's smile vanished and she glared at Blade, who ignored her. Nebon Bossir did not miss the exchange or what it meant. "Lord Blade, I thank you. As you have been honest enough to warn me, may I trust you with my safety until my men come up? I would not leave my grandfather alone in his last hours." He spurred his heuda forward, and rode straight through the mounted guards and into the city without a backward glance.

As Nebon vanished, Serana finally got her voice back. She shook herself like a wet dog and said unsteadily, "W—what can this mean, Blade? He—he is here in Morina. Yet—he did not sign our agreement. What are we going to do about him, Blade? What can we do?"

Blade shook his head slowly, trying not to laugh at Serana's confusion. It would be cruel, and besides, he suspected that if he started laughing now he might not be able to stop.

Finally, he said, "I don't know what 'we' are going to do. *I* am not going to be a part of anything you do. I must be on my way. Serana, my lady—Nebon Bossir is going to be *your* problem."

Chapter 23

Just to make everything more complicated, Count Drago Bossir began a miraculous recovery when his long-lost grandson returned. His fever left him, he called for wine and beef, and over the meal he told Nebon of the agreement over the succession to Morina.

Serana was not much happier over Count Drago's recovery than she was over Nebon's return. However, there was nothing she could do about either one, particularly not after Nebon's outlaws moved into the city to guard him.

Perhaps Serana had even given up the thought of doing anything drastic about the Bossirs. Blade certainly hoped so. He did know that she would have very little time for plotting. Morina was a shambles, and there were thousands of wounded, and thousands more widows and orphans. In spite of her ambitions and her bloodthirsty streak, Serana knew her duties to these people.

Repairing the damage of the war would keep Serana busy for quite a while. Making sure Morina got its proper share of the spoils of the war would take even longer. In theory, all the newly independent leaders of Rentoro ought to be overflowing with gratitude to Morina for its heroic stand against the Wolves. In practice, Blade knew that few politicians in any Dimension ever gave anybody anything out of pure gratitude.

By the time Serana had time to think of intrigue, she would probably know Nebon Bossir quite well. Blade expected she could also come to like him. He seemed to be an abler man than his younger brother, or at least a great deal more sophisticated. He lacked Zemun's charm, of course, and he had a bloodthirsty streak that matched Serana's. After five years as the disguised leader of a band of desperate outlaws, he could hardly be gentle and kind. In time he and Serana should be able to marry, and the succession to Morina would be safe. Zemun's son, or theirs, would someday reign as duke—as long as they didn't work off their bloodthirsty streaks on each other!

As an additional precaution, Blade sat down in a long private conference with Haymi Razence. When they rose from the table, Razence understood clearly the need for a third party in Morina, a neutral man who was neither Bossir nor Zotair and had armed men at his command. He was willing to be that third party—and Blade was willing to believe he would do the job well.

Two nights later, Blade saddled up the stoutest heuda he could find in Morina, and rode out of the city. He rode fully armed and armored, and in his belt pouch were half a dozen sky-bridge crystals. His destination was the Wizard's castle, and hopefully the Wizard himself.

Blade rode across a land where law and order were coming apart. It was not pretty to see everyone trying to grab the most from the collapse of the Wizard's rule. At times Blade felt a heavy burden of responsibility for this situation. If he hadn't taken a hand, the Wizard might still be ruling in Rentoro and none of this would be happening.

On the other hand, twenty thousand people in Morina would be dead or slaves in the Wizard's castle and mines. This chaos would also have happened in the Wizard left Rentoro and came back to Home Dimension. In fact, the chaos would have been worse, because the Wolves would still have been strong and determined to fight to the last. Nothing was happening now that wouldn't have happened sooner or later.

Blade rode by night and stayed hidden by day. He rode as fast as he could, avoiding other people as much as possible. He stole his food and drink and fresh heudas, and preferred to outrun bandits and stray Wolves rather than fight them. Few challenged him anyway. He looked too tough and well-armed.

Blade was not sure what he was going to find when he reached the Wizard's palace. He was not even completely sure what he expected to find. Certainly the Wizard would hardly feel grateful toward him. On the other hand, the Wizard had been willing to give up his power for the simple chance of returning to Renaissance Italy and finishing his days as Bernardo Sembruzo, Conde di Pietroverde. If he was sane, he could hardly be ready to strike down Blade merely for ending the power that he himself had been so willing to give up.

But was he sane? Suppose a madman waited in the Wizard's castle? A madman, whose power to reach and enslave other people's minds might still be intact?

Then Blade might be riding to his death. He fingered the hilt of his dagger. His original decision still stood. Death would be better than letting the Wizard get control of his mind. It would be a grim and foolish irony to have to kill himself now, after living through the battle of Morina. It would be still worse to become the Wizard's mental slave, living in a shadow world created by his master. In time the Rentorans might storm the castle, slay the Wizard, and free the body of Richard Blade. He doubted they would also be able to free his mind. Far better a quick, clean death here and now.

It was normally two weeks' travel from Morina to the Wizard's castle. Blade made the journey in ten days, in spite of the disorder spreading across Rentoro. The "armies" sent out by the cities and towns were hardly more than mobs, and Blade usually found it easy to give them a wide berth.

The few times he got close to one of them, he had a mild surprise. Three times he saw men in unmistakable Wolf armor, just as unmistakably giving orders and being obeyed. Why not? Blade thought. The Wolves were about the only people in Rentoro with real military training. Vengeance was all very well in its place, but someone was certain to realize that the Wolves were too valuable to kill. Then the Wolves in turn must have realized they had a skill to sell, or at least trade for their lives. Blade wondered if in time the surviving Wolves would emerge as a regular class of professional mercenaries, like the *condottieri* of Renaissance Italy. The Wizard would appreciate that final irony, if he managed to be around to see it!

As Blade approached the Wizard's territory, the marching armies faded away and even the refugees and bandits became fewer. Most of the people around here seemed to be already dead or else scattered to whatever safety they could find elsewhere in Rentoro. The few Blade talked to spoke of a terrible curse fallen on the Wizard's castle—fire, thunder, plague, Wolves and servants alike going mad. Blade did not believe all the stories, but it certainly seemed that something ugly

170

had been going on at the castle. He began to wonder if the Wizard was still alive.

On the ninth day he was only a few miles north of Peloff, and he decided to risk pressing on in the daylight. That brought him another surprise, much greater than seeing Wolves leading Rentoro's armies and much more pleasant.

He was trotting through an orchard when suddenly a shout ahead made him pull up. Then five helmeted heads rose from behind a stone wall on the far side of the orchard. A woman's head rose beside them, and at the sight of her Blade stopped his wild grab for his sword.

"Lorya! What are you doing here?"

Lorya laughed and whispered quickly in the ear of one of the men. He motioned to his followers to lay down their weapons, and all five men crowded around Blade's heuda. Lorya stood to one side, and Blade saw that she was now tanned and toughened like leather, her hair cut even shorter than before. She wore a loose tunic and baggy trousers, and no on would have taken her for a woman, except for one thing. Her swordbelt was let out to its last notch to accomodate an unmistakable swelling of her waist.

Then Blade became aware that one of the five men was taking off his helmet and bowing his head. "Lord Blade," he said. "Your Chosen Woman Lorya has been of our band these past months. It was not her belief that she would see you again. Is it your wish that she return to you?"

Blade shook his head. He wasn't sure what was going on here, but he knew Lorya was *not* coming with him this time. "No. I have business with the Wizard himself." Instead of staring, the men nodded as if they understood perfectly what Blade meant. He went on. "I cannot take a woman with child into such danger. No, Lorya has found worthy protection here among you. Let this continue."

"We are honored, Lord Blade," said the leader. "Will you honor us further by spending the night at our camp?" Blade looked at Lorya for some clue as to what he should answer and saw her nod. She seemed to be trying not to burst out laughing. He would come to the camp, all right—and the first thing he'd do there was get Lorya's story from her. He'd never quite accepted the idea of her being dead—but he'd certainly never expected to find her alive, well, and giving orders to armed men.

That night, over beer and fresh-killed venison, she told him

171

her tale. When the fifteen days of Peloff were over, she waited five more. Then she rode west to a farm. The people there took her in, and believed her tale of being under the protection of a great wizard, the Lord Blade, who had come from a distant land to meet the Wizard of Rentoro.

This tale did more than gain her good treatment at the farm. It prepared the farmer and his neighbors for the events that followed. When the rumors ran across the land that the Wolves were on the march and Morina was rising against the Wizard, they knew what was happening. The Lord Blade and the Wizard had fallen out, and their great duel would bring the Wizard's rule in Rentoro to an end.

By now Lorya had taken the farmer's second son as her lover, and she persuaded him to organize the young men of all the nearby farms as a band of warriors. It did not matter who won, she said—they would have to protect themselves, and neither side could punish them for that. It took some time for a century of fear of the Wizard to vanish, but in the end the job was done.

So now Lorya's lover commanded forty men, half of them mounted, and they patrolled the country for many miles in all directions. They kept the Wolves and the bandits out, and collected some taxes of their own. Lorya herself had learned to use a sword until she was a useful member of the band. Of course, in another month or so she would have to start saving her strength for the baby—

She saw the question in Blade's eyes and nodded. "It is yours."

"Does your lover know?"

"Yes. I made him swear a mighty oath to treat the Lord Blade's seed as he would treat the Lord Blade himself."

"And if he breaks that oath?"

"He is not the only protector in Rentoro. If I find a man who is traveling to Dodini, I may go with him anyway. I do not know what is happening in Dodini, but I do not think anyone there will now punish me for defying the Wizard!"

"That seems likely enough," said Blade. "Lorya, you've done rather well by yourself. I wish you luck—"

"No, Blade," she said with a smile. "Wish that I go on making my own luck. That is what you told me to do when you sent me to Peloff. That is what I have been doing."

Blade couldn't argue. He only hoped she could go on making this kind of luck as long as she needed to—long enough to get home to Dodini, long enough for Rentoro to settle down. She deserved to live, and Rentoro needed more cool heads like hers.

Chapter 24

The next morning Blade kissed Lorya farewell, thanked her lover for his hospitality, and rode off to the south. With him as he rode was the knowledge that before dark tonight he might be confronting the Wizard.

In Peloff he saw again what might have happened to Lorya if she hadn't done so well making her own luck. There was no Peloff now, only ashes, charred timbers, and blackened stone. Bodies lay in the streets, most so badly charred that neither decay nor scavengers had touched them. Blade skirted the edge of the town and kept on to the south.

The village on the border of the Wizard's land still stood, but there was not a living human being in it, or a dead one either. Only flies on the garbage heaps and a scavenger dog or two moved among the houses and inns. The people might have evaporated, like dew at sunrise.

Blade climbed to the top of one of the inns and scanned the countryside to the south. He could see no one at work in the fields and no Wolves patrolling the roads, but neither surprised him. The Wolves and everyone else who could get clear of the Wizard's land must have long since done so.

If they could get clear. Everyone he'd met on the road spoke of something terrible and violent happening in the castle. Rumor and panic could exaggerate, but Blade wondered if they could make up such a tale out of thin air. He'd hoped he was through with mysteries in Rentoro, yet here he was, faced with one more!

Blade went downstairs and found dry bread and stale cheese. The water in the well was still clean. He drank and filled his water bottle. Then he mounted his heuda and rode south, past the white posts into the Wizard's empty lands.

In all the miles to the castle Blade did not meet a single living human being. The Wizard's lands seemed to have been depopulated as completely and as mysteriously as the village

174

on the border. Blade began to hope for the sight of a burned house or a sprawled body, anything to tell of ordinary human violence. He had the feeling that he was riding down the road under the eyes of a thousand watchful ghosts.

Whatever had happened to the Wizard's people, it had happened some time ago. Kitchen gardens were rank with weeds. Livestock wandered aimlessly, browsing on the standing grain, while unmilked cows bellowed in agony.

Mile after mile without a sign of life, with all the defensible points abandoned. The bridges were intact, the fortified houses empty, not a single sentry visible anywhere. Now an army of ten thousand men could march up to the walls of the castle in a single day. Did the Wizard care?

By the time the castle loomed on the horizon ahead, Blade was almost certain his journey was in vain. The Wizard was dead. He had to be. He'd driven his people off, or perhaps killed them, and then ended his own life somehow. He was gone and all his secrets with him.

Yet Blade was not going to accept this idea until he'd explored the castle and seen the Wizard's body with his own eyes.

Blade rode up to the same gate he'd entered before and found it standing wide open. He rode straight in through the gateway and turned to the right. That led to the normal route into the castle. The booby traps and other devices along the route that had tested him and trained the Wolves might have broken down—and they might not have. Blade wasn't going to take any unnecessary chances, this close to his goal.

He found two half-decayed bodies on his way in. They lay on the path side by side, a Wolf and what must have once been a young woman. The Wolf's skeletal hand clutched the hilt of a sword driven through the woman's body. Apparently she'd been fleeing when the Wolf overtook her. Fleeing from what? And why was the Wolf dead beside her? There was no sign of violence on the body or on the rusty armor that still encased it.

Blade rode on, and shortly before dark tied his heuda to the knocker on the innermost gate. Then he tied his pouch with the sky-bridge crystals to his belt. He didn't want to leave anything as valuable on the heuda, just in case the castle was not as deserted as it looked.

The gate was closed but not locked. Blade pushed it open and slipped inside. A few feet beyond the gate he nearly stumbled over another body. This one was almost fresh, and wore the robe of one of the Wizard's assistants. A faint gleam of metal caught Blade's eye. He bent down and saw one of the Wizard's own jeweled daggers thrust up to the hilt in the young man's back. Blade pulled it out and added it to the pouch on his belt.

A narrow dark passageway led to the courtyard in front of the Great Hall. Blade came to the end of the passageway and stopped abruptly. In the center of the courtyard the stones were cracked and blackened, in one spot melted into blackish glass. All around the blackened area lay bodies. A few were slightly burned, but most were intact and fairly fresh. Nearly all the bodies were naked, and some of the men and women lay locked together. A barrel of wine had split apart and dumped its contents across the stones, and drinking cups, robes, armor, and daggers lay scattered everywhere. It looked to Blade as if a sort of open-air orgy had been suddenly, gruesomely, and fatally interrupted.

Blade finished examining the courtyard, then raised his eyes to the window of the Great Hall. Half of it was gone, blown out by whatever had interrupted the orgy and fallen in pieces on the stone below. The pale glow of a lantern was visible at the bottom of the window, and Blade thought he saw a human head silhouetted against the glow. Slowly he stepped out into the open courtyard, and as he did the head turned and Blade heard a familiar voice call out:

"Ho, Blade! Come up. I have much to say to you."

It was the Wizard.

The man sounded perfectly normal, not even angry, but Blade still preferred to be careful. The normal route to the Great Hall would give anyone waiting for him a dozen opportunities to lay ambushes in the darkness. So Blade scrambled up the wall beneath the window, using his rock-climbing skills on the carved cornices and gargoyles. He found an entire section of window knocked cleanly out and swung himself in through it, dropping into combat stance the moment his feet hit the floor.

The Wizard showed no surprise at seeing Blade come in through the window instead of the door. He was sitting at a table under the window, with a view-ball in front of him. It was activated—Blade caught a glimpse of blue sky and stark, snow-crested mountains. Beside the view-ball lay a yard-long wooden stick with a silver ball on one end.

The Wizard rose and came forward to greet Blade. There was new gray hair at his temples and his eyes were red, but otherwise he seemed as vigorous and well-groomed as ever. Blade took three backward steps and drew his sword. "If you don't mind, I'd rather you didn't come any closer."

The Wizard stopped and laughed softly. "So we are back to the first moves of our game, are we?"

"Yes, until I know what the game is."

"Ah, it will not take long to tell you." The Wizard's voice was low, his words were clear, and Blade could detect no sign of strain, tension, or loss of control in the man. He would almost have felt better if the Wizard had been raving and drooling. Under the circumstances, the man's calm was unnatural, even frightening.

"You surprised me when you and Serana fled that night," said the Wizard. "It was not a pleasant surprise, either. But when I thought over all you had done and said, I saw the truth clearly for the first time. Your destiny would not be linked to mine, at least not in Rentoro. So it was time to change my plans. My power would pass from Rentoro when I did, so what further use were my people?"

"You mean the Wolves?"

"Yes, and all the others as well. They had no further purpose. So the Wolves went against Morina, and did as well as they could without my aid. I would have been happier if Morina had perished along with the Wolves, but much was accomplished in spite of this failure."

"Not all the Wolves are dead," said Blade. "Some are finding places as leaders of Rentoro's new armies." Perhaps it was not wise to say this, and certainly he didn't like the Wolves any better than before. Nonetheless he was disgusted by the Wizard's sending out his faithful Wolves to be slaughtered simply because he could not stand the idea of his people living on after him.

"Ah," the Wizard said. "I would deal with them if I could, but the time for that is past. I have no one left to help me, unless you—no, I see that you would not care to, as much as you seem to have hated the Wolves."

"You are quite right," said Blade. "But where are the rest of your people? The castle seems to be deserted, except for a few bodies. Did they flee, or—"

"They did not flee," said the Wizard quietly. He rested a hand on the view-ball and concentrated all his attention on the image. It dissolved, the view-ball seemed to become filled with boiling milk, then a new image started to form.

Blade was strongly tempted to take advantage of the Wizard's concentration and knock him unconscious. He did not like what the Wizard's story implied about the man's state of mind. A feeling was growing in him that the Wizard should *not* be taken back to Home Dimension, even if it turned out to be possible. Was the Wizard still capable of revealing his secrets and teaching his skills? Perhaps. But wasn't he even more likely to prove murderously dangerous? Sooner or later he would be stopped, but at what cost to the Project? What cost in lives? The more Blade thought about it, the idea of bringing the Wizard home seemed like bringing a man-eating tiger to a cocktail party.

Then the new image was formed in the view-ball, and the Wizard raised his hand to give Blade a clear look at it. Blade stared—and although he'd thought he was past being surprised or shocked by anything in Rentoro, his jaw dropped.

He saw the rugged, snow-covered surface of what seemed to be an endless glacier. Far off on the horizon jagged mountain peaks thrust up against a gray sky. The snow flew up in clouds, lashed by an icy wind.

The surface of the glacier was covered with frozen contorted bodies, both men and women. Blade recognized the clothes of castle servants and farm laborers, the armor of household guards and Wolves. Among the bodies a few living people crawled on all fours, like animals. With knives and bare hands they tore at the corpses all around them and crammed the frozen flesh into their mouths.

Blade forced his eyes away from the view-ball, but he could not quite make himself look at the Wizard. "You sent them all to the north?" he said, in a distant voice.

"Yes," said the Wizard. "Many years ago I went into the frozen mountains beyond the crystal mines and placed sky-bridge crystals there. I thought I might someday need a road of escape. Every year I went back there and saw that the crystals were still sound.

"Then the end did come. You brought it. Those who had served me could not be permitted to live, yet I could not kill them all myself. So I opened the sky-bridge into the north. I told all my people they would pass across it to safety, in a land where no one would know them. They obeyed—"

"Not all of them."

"No. There were some who rebelled, because they did not trust me. They had to be slain here in the castle. But most went across the sky-bridge, and now they are all dead or dying. Those who still live eat the flesh of the dead. Not even the bodies will be found, for they will vanish into the glacier and the glacier into the sea. To Rentoro, it will be as if all those who served in my castle and on my lands vanished into the sky. I did not leave Morina as a monument to my power, but I will leave this memory." The Wizard's voice was beginning to rise. Blade found it hard to keep his hands steady. They were shaking with his efforts to keep them from closing around the Wizard's throat and squeezing.

"Then I destroyed the sky-bridge, and by the power of my mind alone slew all those who had remained behind to guard it. You saw their bodies in the courtyard. Now only you and I remain alive in all the castle, and soon we also shall be gone. You will return to your England, and I will return with you. You have not served me here in Rentoro, but you will in England, and you will be the first of many to serve me there."

With those last words, the Wizard snatched up the stick from the table and smashed it across Blade's sword arm. Blade felt the bone go and saw the sword fly across the room. He started to draw his dagger with his left hand, then suddenly the Wizard was assaulting his mind more strongly than ever before.

Without the moment's warning given by the Wizard's physical attack, Blade's mind would have been in the other man's grip in seconds. He staggered back, both hands dropping limply, unable to even think about drawing his dagger. He took two more backward steps, then the Wizard's mental commands forced him to stop. He began to concentrate all his attention on simply keeping his mind out of the Wizard's grip, letting his body take care of itself.

The Wizard had gained in mental power since Blade left the castle. This was clear within moments. Blade ran through his mind mathematical formulas, images of London, images of his travels and battles in Rentoro and elsewhere. The Wizard matched every formula and image with one of his own that quickly dominated Blade's. Blade felt like a small radio station jammed by a more powerful one. He was grimly aware that he had no more than a few minutes of mental

179

freedom left. The Wizard was going to beat him down, and then—

Then he would do his best to return to Home Dimension with Blade, and he might succeed. He might arrive there with Blade firmly under his control and unable to warn anyone. Then the tiger would be loose in the cocktail party. The Wizard's dreams of ruling England were the ravings of a madman. But how many people would die before the Wizard was stopped, and what would happen to Project Dimension X?

Blade knew he had to kill himself, or at least knock himself unconscious. He might end up staying here in Rentoro, the mind-slave of the Wizard until the man was killed, but that would be better than loosing the Wizard on an unsuspecting Home Dimension.

He forced himself to take a step toward the window. The Wizard increased his attacks. Blade tried to take another step and found his legs giving under him. He fell to his hands and knees, gasping, his head beginning to throb painfully with the effort of fighting the Wizard.

Then the throbbing in his head became the familiar pain that told of Lord Leighton's computer reaching out to grip his brain. It was agony, but at this moment it was also the most glorious sensation Blade could remember feeling. He would go Home, alive, his mind free, and be damned to the Wizard and his secrets!

Then the Wizard staggered and clapped both hands to his temples, crying out, "Blade! My head!" The room began to swirl around Blade, and only the Wizard remained clear, fighting to stay on his feet, eyes shut and face contorted.

The mental link between them meant the computer was gripping the Wizard's brain too! He *was* going to come back to Home Dimension with Blade, unless Blade could break the link. He tried to turn around, found his feet rooted to the floor, managed to draw his dagger, raised it, took a step forward—

—and then everything dissolved into thundering black swirling chaos, with red and gold flaming through it. Blade fell through the chaos, the Wizard fell beside him, and suddenly there was a hard floor under Blade. He heard his dagger clatter on stone, saw the chair in the glass booth looming over him, and heard Leighton's voice.

"He's back—and there's someone with him!"

Blade saw the Wizard sprawled unconscious on the other side of the chair and knew he had to speak. He raised his head and croaked, "Dangerous—telepath—mad—killed all—"

Then he felt as if he'd been hit on the back of the head with a club. He slumped forward, and a complete blackness that wasn't chaotic at all but very soothing swallowed him up.

Chapter 25

Slowly Blade drifted back to consciousness. He was in his usual room in the Project's private hospital. J just standing at the foot of the bed, flanked by two attractive nurses. Blade struggled up into a sitting position, discovering in the process that his right arm was in a cast. He looked a question at J.

"Just a simple fracture," the older man said with a smile. "You'll be out of here within a few days, unless the doctors really dig in their heels." J understood what a bad patient Blade was and how he usually recovered faster out of the hospital than in it.

"How is the Wizard?" Blade asked.

"The man who came back with you? We've got him in another room, under sedation. Yes, we heard your warning. We'll keep a close eye on him once he's conscious, although I doubt if an old man like that could really be dangerous, physically or mentally."

"You haven't had any experience of what—" began Blade, then stopped. His mind was still foggy, but somewhere far in the back of it a warning bell was chiming faintly. "Old man?"

"Oh yes—must be as old as Leighton or older. I admit he looked younger when we first saw him. That must have just been a trick of the lighting in the computer room. He—"

Slowly Blade shook his head. "He is younger. Or at least he was. He—"

"Richard, are you all right?"

Blade ignored J. In his mind the warning bell was now clanging like a fire alarm. Ignoring the presence of the nurses, he leaped out of bed and snatched up a hospital gown. The nurses drew back, not quite willing to tackle Blade in this condition without J's permission. Before J could say anything, Blade pulled the gown over his head and was out the door.

He trotted down the corridor as fast as he could go without jarring his broken arm. Then he realized that in his haste he'd forgotten to ask what room the Wizard was in. Before he could turn back, two doctors and three nurses came charging down the corridor at a dead run, carrying every sort of emergency medical gear Blade had ever seen. One of them recognized Blade and snapped, "Get back into bed, for God's sake! We've got a total cardiac arrest in that old man Leighton dumped on us!" Before Blade could reply the medical team vanished into the nearest room.

Blade followed them in. The doctor turned to whisper savagely, "Get out of here, you—" But another doctor pointed at the electroencephalograph standing beside the bed. It showed that all brain function had ceased in the man lying in the bed.

Bernardo Sembruzo, Conde di Pietroverde, captain for the Visconti, Wizard of Rentoro, genius, was dead—dead of the old age his mental powers had kept at bay for so long, until those powers were destroyed by the passage from Rentoro to Home Dimension.

Blade looked down at the wrinkled, shrunken, white-haired thing in the bed, and once again he could not have said a word to save his life. The Wizard had turned all his widom to uses that grew more and more evil, but he'd had that wisdom. He'd had it until Richard Blade—or at least something that Richard Blade set in motion—destroyed it.

In silence Blade walked back to his room, leaving the doctors and nurses standing around the dead Wizard. In spite of his broken arm, his exhaustion, and the sleeping pills the nurses gave him, Blade found it rather hard to get to sleep that night.

Four days later Blade was sitting in a chair in Leighton's private office. J was sitting in another, and Leighton sat behind his great battered Victorian desk. Beside the desk was a rectangular box covered with canvas and a battered briefcase.

Leighton looked up from his desk with a strangely satisfied smile on his face. Blade wasn't sure what there was to be satisfied about, considering that this trip to Rentoro seemed to have been a complete waste for everybody except the Rentorans.

"Ah, Richard," said Lighton cheerfully. "J tells me that

you've been rather depressed over the fate of the Wizard. Blaming yourself for his death and all that."

There were times when J carried his fatherly interest in Blade a little too far. Blade frowned. "I think depressed is too strong a word. However, I will admit that I do feel responsible for a somewhat unfortunate situation." When he chose, Blade could use an understatement as well as anybody. "The Wizard must have had one of the most powerful minds that ever lived. That mind was working, even if rather oddly, until I dragged him with me into Home Dimension."

"The Wizard's situation was already unfortunate before you had anything to do with him," said Leighton. "The autopsy showed that. He'd been able to control the aging process in his body, but only partly in his brain. The autopsy showed a good many brain cells that had lost function long before you came on the scene. He must have already been on the edge, and those last efforts put him over. He was caught in a vicious circle. The more his brain deteriorated, the more wild ideas he got, and the more wild ideas he got, the more he increased the strain and the rate of deterioration.

"No, Richard, there's nothing you did to the Wizard that wasn't already inevitable—and close. In fact, one might say that you gave him a more merciful death than he would have had otherwise. If he hadn't come with you, he would have ended up a mindless animal, staggering, then crawling, then lying in his own filth until he died of thirst or starvation or disease. As it was, he died painlessly in a hospital bed, not even knowing that he was dying."

Blade felt a great sense of relief. If Leighton said this, it was true to the best of his knowledge. Leighton would lie with a perfectly straight face about quite a few things, but never about anything scientific. On scientific questions he would not tell a lie to save himself from a firing squad, let alone to make Richard Blade feel less guilty.

Blade smiled. "So I suppose he would not have been able to teach me or anyone else his skills, even in Rentoro?"

"Unlikely, to say the least. The effort involved in the teaching would probably have pushed him over the edge."

"So now he really is gone, and all his secrets with him," said Blade.

Leighton's eyes sparkled. "Not quite, Richard, not quite." Painfully he bent down and pulled off the canvas cover, revealing a wire cage with two white mice in it. Then he opened the briefcase and took out two pairs of sky-bridge crystals. They were only a fraction of the normal size, but there was no mistaking the material.

Leighton placed one pair carefully on his desk, then put the other pair on the floor in front of the cage. Blade held his breath. Leighton opened the cage door, the mice darted out, they passed between the crystals on the floor—

—then with a faint *pop* they appeared between the crystals on Leighton's desk. Both were lying motionless on their sides, but Leighton reached over and gently prodded their stomachs with a finger. Slowly they got to their feet, then darted for the edge of the desk. J caught them as they reached it, cupped one in each hand, and gently returned them to the cage.

"We are able to cut these from one of the crystals you brought, then activate them electrically," said Leighton. "Unlike mental force, electricity makes the crystals permanently active, and uses them up rather quickly. So we can't make any really high-capacity sky-bridges with the crystals you brought back.

"However, we're working on that. A spectrographic analysis suggests at least the possibility of synthesizing the crystals on a large scale. It will require a fairly large investment in research—don't groan out loud, J, if you please!—but I suspect that in the near future . . ."

Blade found himself unable to pay attention to Leighton's predictions about the near future. A single, magnificently satisfying thought was echoing around his mind.

It hadn't been wasted, after all.

IT'S ALWAYS ACTION WITH

BLADE

HEROIC FANTASY SERIES
by Jeffrey Lord

The continuing saga of a modern man's exploits in the hitherto uncharted realm of worlds beyond our knowledge. Richard Blade is everyman and at the same time, a mighty and intrepid warrior. In the best tradition of America's most popular fictional heroes—giants such as Tarzan, Doc Savage and Conan—

		Title	Book #	Price
———	#1	THE BRONZE AXE	P201	$ .95
———	#2	THE JADE WARRIOR	P593	$1.25
———	#3	JEWEL OF THARN	P203	$ .95
———	#4	SLAVE OF SARMA	P204	$ .95
———	#5	LIBERATOR OF JEDD	P205	$ .95
———	#6	MONSTER OF THE MAZE	P206	$ .95
———	#7	PEARL OF PATMOS	P767	$1.25
———	#8	UNDYING WORLD	P208	$ .95
———	#9	KINGDOM OF ROYTH	P295	$ .95
———	#10	ICE DRAGON	P768	$1.25
———	#11	DIMENSION OF DREAMS	P474	$1.25
———	#12	KING OF ZUNGA	P523	$1.25
———	#13	THE GOLDEN STEED	P559	$1.25
———	#14	THE TEMPLES OF AYOCAN	P623	$1.25
———	#15	THE TOWERS OF MELNON	P688	$1.25
———	#16	THE CRYSTAL SEAS	P780	$1.25
———	#17	THE MOUNTAINS OF BREGA	P812	$1.25
———	#18	WARLORDS OF GAIKON	P822	$1.25
———	#19	LOOTERS OF THARN	P855	$1.25
———	#20	GUARDIANS OF THE CORAL THRONE	P881	$1.25

TO ORDER

Please check the space next to the books/s you want, send this order form together with your check or money order, include the price of the book/s and 25¢ for handling and mailing to:
PINNACLE BOOKS, INC. / P.O. Box 4347
Grand Central Station / New York, N.Y. 10017

☐ CHECK HERE IF YOU WANT A FREE CATALOG

I have enclosed $_____check_____or money order_____as payment in full. No C.O.D.'s.

Name_____

Address_____

City_____State_____Zip_____

(Please allow time for delivery)   PB-35